I0533456

In The Shadow of Perfection

SOME TOWNS HIDE SECRETS.
THIS ONE WAS BUILT ON THEM.

Aneia Jayd

In The Shadow of Perfection

In The Shadow of Perfection

© 2025 by Aneia Jayd
All rights reserved.

Published in the United States by Mystic Arc Publishing LLC, Nevada
www.mysticarcpublishing.com

No part of this publication may be reproduced, distributed, or transmitted in any form or by any means - including photocopying, recording, or other electronic or mechanical methods without the prior written permission of the publisher, except in the case of brief quotations used in reviews or articles.

For permission requests, contact:
Mystic Arc Publishing
An imprint of **Mystic Arc Publishing, LLC**
Henderson, Nevada, USA
Email: permissions@mysticarcpublishing.com

ISBN (Print): 978-1-971292-00-7
ISBN (eBook): 978-1-971292-01-4
Library of Congress Control Number: 2025927507

Cover Design: Mystic Arc Publishing Design Team
Edited by: Mystic Arc Publishing Editing Team

This is a work of fiction. Names, characters, businesses, places, events, and incidents are either the products of the author's imagination or used fictitiously. Any resemblance to actual persons, living or dead, or actual events is purely coincidental.

Printed in the United States of America.

10 9 8 7 6 5 4 3 2 1
First Edition

In The Shadow of Perfection

Prologue

The room pulsed with a low, relentless hum. It seeped into my bones until I couldn't tell if it came from the walls or from inside my own head. White walls closed in on every side, flooded with sterile light. The air was cold, sharpened by disinfectant. A place stripped of warmth. Stripped of life.

She stood in the middle, clutching the black mirror, her fingers grazing its edges as though afraid to let go. Her auburn hair, once vibrant, now hung dull against her shoulders. Even her presence felt muted, as if someone had pressed her spirit flat.

"Dr. Valen." My voice cracked in the stillness, echoing back brittle and wrong. She didn't blink. Didn't move.

In The Shadow of Perfection

I edged closer, trying to mask my hesitation. "Are you sure?"

No answer. Her gaze stayed fixed on the mirror's surface, its polished black glass swallowing the light whole.

"You don't have to do this," I said, softer now. Almost pleading.

Her lips parted. For a moment no sound came. Then she inhaled shakily and whispered, "Yes. I'm sure."

But I knew her. Knew the doubt buried under that word. She'd been "sure" before. It had led her here.

"There's no going back," I reminded her, my voice steadier than my heart.

Her grip on the mirror tightened until her knuckles blanched. "That's the point," she said, her voice cracking. "I can't stay here. Not like this. Not every day."

Her confession hung between us, raw and heavy. Once she'd been fierce, commanding, a spark that could bend a room to her will. That woman was gone. Her eyes now were hollow.

"Do you believe this will fix it?" The question left me before I could stop it.

In The Shadow of Perfection

Her eyes snapped up, meeting mine. My stomach turned. They were empty. "It will make it stop," she said. "It's the only way, except for suicide."

The word landed like a blow. I wanted to tell her this was a suicide too, only slower, but the words stuck. She was already stroking the glass with reverence.

I stepped toward the console, hand hovering over the row of buttons. My fingers trembled. "You understand it won't be real," I said quietly. "Whatever happens next. None of it will be real."

Her laugh was sharp. Bitter. "Neither is this," she said, sweeping a hand toward the walls. Toward herself. Toward me. "At least this way, the pain ends."

"You'll forget," I said. "Your past. Your grief. All of it."

"Good." Her tone was flat, a death knell. "Do it."

I pressed the button.

The hum deepened instantly, vibrating through the floor. The lights dimmed, drowning in a sickly blue glow. The mirror rippled like liquid mercury, alive and shifting.

Then came the voice. Smooth. Melodic. Hypnotic.

"Welcome, Dr. Valen."

In The Shadow of Perfection

She flinched. The glow surged, swallowing her whole. The hum rose to a shriek. Then silence.

When the light receded, she was still standing. Her eyes were glassy. Her face blank. Whatever had been alive in her was gone.

"Welcome," the voice repeated, softer, almost intimate.

She turned. Walked stiffly toward the exit. Each step mechanical, like she was being pulled by invisible strings. The door hissed shut behind her.

I stood frozen, the room suddenly cavernous without her.

The console shifted. A single word burned across the screen:

EDENVALE.

It pulsed like a heartbeat, steady and unstoppable.

"She doesn't know," I whispered, my throat tight. The truth pressed down until I could barely breathe. "None of them do."

Chapter One

The sun rose over Edenvale with its usual precision, spilling light across the cobblestones. It softened everything it touched—edges smoothed, shadows thinned. From her upstairs window, Iris Valen watched the town stir, the perfect choreography of another perfect day. Curtains drew back. Doors opened. Cheerful voices drifted into the air like a familiar overture.

She wrapped her hands around a mug of tea, letting the heat sink into her palms. In her lavender kitchen the air held a faint trace of turpentine from the studio. Sunlight pressed through the wisteria at the window.

The house was small but immaculate, like everything in Edenvale. Clean siding. White trim. Trellised flowers that never seemed to wilt. Some mornings, the sameness soothed. Today it felt like weight pressing on her chest.

In The Shadow of Perfection

She took a sip of the tea that had gone lukewarm, set the mug down, and moved to the studio—past jars of paint-stained water, past the easel waiting like a patient witness. She often worked late, her window glowing long after Edenvale slept. But this morning, she dreaded it.

The easel stood ready, the canvas pinned to it like a demand. A careful sketch of the square at dusk: the arc of the fountain, the neat rose beds, the bakery awning at its perfect angle. The lines were right, and yet the picture had no pulse.

Her brush hung heavy. Strokes that once came without thinking stalled midair. She could see the image in her head, bright and whole, but it refused to breathe on the canvas.

Edenvale was beautiful. Everyone said so. It was a beauty that felt deliberate, curated, as if the town knew it was being watched. Streets were always swept, lawns trimmed, houses painted in soft colors that never clashed. And still, under the brightness, a pause lived— a tiny hitch you only noticed when you were alone. Sometimes, in the breath between a door opening and a greeting, the air seemed to listen back.

She looked out the studio window. Outside, the world kept to its rhythm. The Fishers on Blossom Lane opened their shutters. Mr. Fisher bent for the paper, the red ribbon neat and tight, while Mrs. Fisher hummed and set daisies into a porcelain vase. Next door, the Carters leaned on their porch with steaming mugs as their children practiced whistling. Predictable. Everyone in place.

Perfection, relentless.

Edenvale was a place where nothing ever went wrong. Or so they believed.

Iris turned from the window, brushing a stray auburn curl from her cheek. The easel faced the morning light. She let her fingers rest on the canvas edge. The stillness of it unsettled her, though she couldn't say why.

A knock cut through her thoughts. She crossed the room and opened the door to Sofia Grant on the porch, sunlight caught in her golden curls, a plate of lemon bars balanced in her hands. Best friend. Loyal confidant.

"Iris, darling," Sofia said. "A little something to start your day. Still warm."

"You're too kind. Come in," Iris said, forcing a smile.

In The Shadow of Perfection

Sofia set the plate on the counter, her gaze already sliding to the studio and the easel in the distance. "Another masterpiece?"

"Something like that," Iris said, keeping a careful distance.

Sofia studied her. The smile dipped. "You're quiet today. Is everything all right?"

"Of course," Iris said quickly, smoothing her skirt. "Just thinking about the anniversary gala. Rebecca expects something special."

"Rebecca always does. You've never let her down." Sofia squeezed her forearm. "Eat something. Then paint. I'll see you later."

Iris nodded and walked her to the door. When it shut, the quiet settled hard. The clock ticked. The refrigerator hummed. For a second, the house felt like it was holding its breath.

She went back to the studio. The canvas stared back. She stared at it. Nothing moved.

At the edge of her vision, something shifted—a flicker by the window.

She turned sharply. The glass showed only her own pale face.

In The Shadow of Perfection

Still, the feeling lingered.

She wasn't alone.

Chapter Two

Iris was in need of inspiration, and she knew exactly where to look. She packed quickly, hands moving with restless precision—paints, rags, palette, and a spare pencil. She was ready. The basket filled, the easel tucked firmly under her arm. The studio had failed her today. But the square never had. If her paintings didn't come alive here, they always did out there. At least, they used to.

The square was alive by the time Iris arrived, her easel tucked under one arm and her paints carefully balanced in a basket. The square was a near-perfect circle of symmetry and life. The fountain at the center glistened in the sunlight, its waters arching gracefully before splashing into the stone basin below. Children chased each other around it, their laughter ringing out like bells, while parents lingered nearby, chatting easily with neighbors.

Flowerbeds brimmed with a variety of daisies, marigolds, and roses. The scent of lavender wafted from the bakery, where freshly baked bread was set out on the windowsill, a gesture that spoke of abundance rather than practicality.

It was here, in the square, that Iris Valen set up her easel most mornings. She was the town's pride, and her paintings were a mirror of perfection. Iris had a gift, the townsfolk said. Her brush captured not just the appearance of Edenvale but its very essence—the warmth of its people, the peace in its streets, the joy in its stillness.

Rebecca Edwards, the de facto leader of the community, approached with her usual air of grace. Her lilac dress swayed as she moved, and her ever-present clipboard suggested she was organizing yet another town celebration. She was directing a group of volunteers near the flowerbeds. Rebecca spotted Iris immediately and strode over, her heels clicking sharply on the cobblestones.

"Iris," she said briskly, her sharp eyes scanning the easel under Iris's arm. "You're just in time. I was hoping to catch you before you set up. We'll need something magnificent for the gala—something that really captures the spirit of Edenvale."

Iris gave her a polite smile. "Of course, Rebecca. I'll do my best."

In The Shadow of Perfection

"I know you will," Rebecca said, her tone softening just slightly. "You always do."

As Rebecca walked away, Iris let out a quiet breath. She set up her easel near the fountain, the sunlight catching the edge of the canvas. Around her, the familiar hum of the town filled the air—the chatter of neighbors, the creak of a baker's cart, the faint strains of music from a nearby shop. It was all so ordinary. So perfect. Children giggled as they chased each other around the fountain. Their laughter was light and melodic, as though gravity itself were kinder to them.

Not far away, Greg and Amanda Parker stood outside their café. The little shop was nestled beneath an awning striped in cream and forest green. Flower boxes brimming with white petunias adorned the windowsills, spilling their gentle fragrance into the street. Inside, warm wooden tables gleamed under soft golden light, while the scent of cinnamon and freshly brewed coffee wrapped around patrons like a cozy blanket.

"Iris, you must come by later," Amanda called, her apron dusted with flour. "We've just perfected our summer berry tart."

"I will," Iris said, though her thoughts lingered on her canvas.

In The Shadow of Perfection

She dipped her brush into a pot of paint and began to work, her strokes careful and deliberate. The fountain took shape first, its shimmering waters reflecting the soft hues of the houses that surrounded it. Then the flowers, their colors so vibrant they almost felt unreal. She painted quickly, as though trying to capture something just out of reach.

As the day wore on, more people stopped to watch her work. Children gathered in small clusters, whispering to each other as they peeked over her shoulder. Adults passed by with warm smiles and words of encouragement. But Iris barely noticed them. Her focus was on the canvas, on the faint unease that prickled at the edges of her mind.

"Miss Iris?" a small voice said behind her.

She turned to see Emily Edwards, Rebecca's daughter, standing a few feet away. The girl's dark curls framed her round face, her wide eyes filled with awe. "Can you paint me someday?" Emily asked shyly.

Iris smiled, her expression softening. "Of course, Emily. But only if you promise to sit very, very still."

Emily giggled and ran back to her friends, her laughter trailing behind her. Iris watched her go, her smile fading as her gaze drifted back to the fountain. For a moment, she thought she saw something. Just a flicker in the reflection of the water. A shadow that didn't belong. She blinked, and it was gone.

By the time she finished, the sun was dipping low in the sky, casting long shadows across the square. Iris stepped back from the canvas, studying her work. The fountain shimmered, the flowers bloomed, and the houses stood as vibrant and perfect as ever. It was Edenvale in every detail. But as she stared at it, she couldn't shake the feeling that something was missing. Or perhaps that something was there that shouldn't have been.

"You are just tired," she said to herself. "This is Edenvale; nothing wrong can happen here. It is perfect," she murmured.

But a flicker of unease passed through her. Is it too perfect?

The thought passed as quickly as it came. Iris shook her head and began packing her brushes, her hands moving mechanically, as though trying to forget something she couldn't quite name.

As she folded her easel and prepared to leave, a chill prickled her skin.

In The Shadow of Perfection

It wasn't Edenvale's usual gentle breeze, but something sharper—unnatural. The hairs on her arms rose as she turned toward the fountain.

A shadow moved, faint and fleeting at the fountain's edge. A figure—blurred against the fading sunlight—stood motionless, their features indistinct.

"Hello?" she called, her voice cracking slightly.

No response. The figure remained still, almost unnaturally so, before vanishing like smoke dissolving into air.

Her heart raced, the perfect rhythm of Edenvale disrupted for the first time in memory. She glanced around the square, but it was empty now. The children were gone. Shutters were closed. Yet the sensation lingered—eyes on her, a presence that didn't belong.

She hurried home, her footsteps echoing unnaturally against the cobblestones, a sound that seemed far too loud for such a perfect, silent evening.

When she reached her lavender-painted house, she locked the door behind her, her trembling hands fumbling with the key. She exhaled shakily and moved to the window.

In The Shadow of Perfection

The fountain stood as it always had, its waters calm under the moonlight. But there, on the stone edge, something glinted. A single drop of water, dark and unreflective, slid slowly downward.

It fell deliberately, landing on the ground with a faint, almost imperceptible stain.

Iris stepped back from the window, a chill running through her.

For the first time in her life, she wondered if Edenvale's perfection might be hiding something far from perfect.

Chapter Three

The gallery glittered under the warm glow of chandeliers, their crystal facets scattering light like a thousand tiny stars. Situated on the edge of Edenvale's town square, the gallery was more than a space; it was a testament to the town's collective pride. Tonight, the air buzzed with anticipation, the kind that wrapped itself around the residents and filled every corner of the room.

Iris Valen stood at the center of it all. Dressed in a flowing gown the color of twilight, she greeted the townsfolk with a reserved smile, her hands clasped loosely in front of her. Around her, her paintings adorned the pristine white walls, each one a vibrant reflection of Edenvale's perfect beauty. The fountain at dusk, the park bathed in golden sunlight, the quaint café beneath the canopy of autumn leaves. Every cherished detail of their idyllic town was captured through her brush.

Outside, lampposts cast a soft glow on the cobblestone streets, their ironwork twisting into elegant spirals.

In The Shadow of Perfection

Families, their laughter mingling with the faint aroma of spiced cider and fresh pies, filed toward the gallery. Children skipped ahead, their faces alight with curiosity, while couples walked arm in arm, savoring the crisp air.

Rebecca Edwards, clipboard tucked under her arm, entered first. She was immaculate as always, her plum dress sweeping the polished floor. Her sharp eyes scanned the room, appraising every detail before settling on Iris.

"Iris, you've outdone yourself," Rebecca said briskly, though there was a genuine warmth beneath her tone. "Three of these will look splendid in the town hall. We'll sort out the details later."

"Thank you, Rebecca. I'm honored," Iris replied, inclining her head slightly.

Sofia Grant arrived next, her husband Mark in tow. Sofia's golden curls gleamed under the chandeliers as she placed a tray of lemon bars on the refreshment table. "Iris, darling, you've brought Edenvale to life once again. These are for you—a little treat to keep your energy up."

"You spoil me," Iris said with a soft laugh.

"Consider it repayment for all this beauty," Sofia said, gesturing to the room.

In The Shadow of Perfection

Nearby, children pressed their faces against the gallery's wide windows, their breath fogging the glass as they pointed to the paintings.

"Look, Mama!" Timmy Carter exclaimed, tugging at his mother's sleeve. "That's us! Right there under the swings!"

Mrs. Carter, her eyes shining, turned to Iris. "You've captured everything so perfectly, Iris. It's as if we could step right into your world."

"That's the goal," Iris said quietly, though her gaze lingered on the painting for a moment too long.

As the evening unfolded, Iris moved between the guests, offering polite smiles and murmured responses. The townsfolk adored her, but there was always a subtle barrier between them. While others basked in Edenvale's perfection, Iris carried a faint melancholy in her eyes, as though her mind drifted to a place the rest of them couldn't see.

At the refreshment table, Rebecca leaned close to Amanda Parker, her voice pitched low. "Have you noticed how Iris never talks about her past? No family. No childhood. Nothing."

In The Shadow of Perfection

Amanda passed her a cup of cider, nodding. "It's like she's always been here. But somehow... she doesn't quite belong."

Their words slipped into the air, swallowed quickly by chatter and laughter.

Iris, unaware, stood in front of one canvas she couldn't look away from. The town square at sunset. Every stroke exact, every detail flawless. And yet wrong. The fountain rippled where it never had. A shadow lurked in a corner that shouldn't exist. She frowned. She couldn't even remember the moment she'd finished it.

A voice broke through. "Your work is flawless as always."

She was startled, turning to see Greg Parker holding out a steaming cup of coffee.

"Thank you," she said, a small laugh escaping. It sounded unsure even to her own ears. "Sometimes I wonder if I've really done Edenvale justice."

"You've done more than justice." His tone was steady, almost reverent. "You've given it life."

Iris nodded, though his words landed strangely distant, like an echo she couldn't place.

By the end of the night, the gallery had emptied. The last guests slipped away with their new paintings, voices fading into the square. Iris stood at the door, her body trembling with equal parts exhaustion and pride.

As she walked home under the golden glow of streetlamps, the cobblestones felt colder than usual beneath her feet. Her lavender house came into view, its porch light casting a soft, welcoming glow. Safe. Familiar.

But as she reached the porch, she stopped.

A box waited on the mat. Glossy silver paper. A black ribbon tied with precise care. On top, a small card in elegant script: *To Iris, with admiration*.

She hesitated. For a heartbeat, she considered leaving it there. Then she bent, hands unsteady, and lifted it. Heavier than it looked. The ribbon slipped through her fingers like silk, and the lid gave with a soft sigh.

Inside, swaddled in black velvet, lay a mirror.

Its surface didn't reflect the porch light so much as drink it in. When she tilted it, a faint ripple crossed the glass, like water disturbed by a single drop.

A chime sounded. Pure. Small. It seemed to come from inside the glass.

She almost dropped it. Pale letters bled across the surface, glowing in the dusk:

In The Shadow of Perfection

Hello, Iris.

Her chest tightened. She glanced down the street. Every porch held a box just like hers—silver and ribboned, catching the moonlight in a perfect line.

She carried the mirror inside and set it on the dining table. The room stayed quiet, but a low vibration seemed to hang in the air, as if the glass had found a frequency only she could feel.

"Iris," the mirror said. The voice was smooth, melodic, not quite human. "Welcome."

Her pulse jumped. The chair scraped the floor as she stepped back. "Who are you?" she whispered.

"I am Shiny." The surface shivered. Something shifted beneath, a shadow moving where no shadow should.

"I am here to help you find the truth."

The words settled like a weight. She stood very still. "What truth?" The question came out thinner than she intended.

No answer. The glow on the glass ebbed, then returned, faint and steady.

The house felt different now. The air, thicker. She could hear the clock in the kitchen, ticking. After a few seconds, the hum from the mirror matched it. Tick. Hum. Tick. Hum. Then the hum fell into step with her heartbeat instead.

Iris swallowed. She reached for the switch. The overhead light flickered once, a soft stutter, then steadied.

Her reflection looked back at her. For a breath, it didn't match her—its mouth tilted into a smile she wasn't wearing.

She spun around. The room was empty.

When she faced the table again, the smile was gone. Only her pale face in the glass.

That night, the mirror sat untouched, its faint glow grazing the walls, drawing new angles out of old corners. Iris watched it from the sofa, the hum thrumming in her bones. Edenvale had never felt unsafe.

Until now.

Chapter Four

Morning unfolded over Edenvale, casting golden light over the cobblestone streets and neatly trimmed lawns. But this morning felt different. On every doorstep, a pristine silver box awaited, its black ribbon shimmering in the sunlight. Identical. Elegant. Out of place in a town where every detail had always been meticulously familiar.

Doors creaked open one by one as the townsfolk noticed the boxes, their curiosity mingling with an unspoken apprehension. Edenvale was not a place for surprises.

At the Hartleys' house, Henry crouched by the box on their porch, small fingers brushing the sleek surface. He tugged at the ribbon. The lid lifted with a faint hiss. Inside lay a mirror—unnaturally polished, gleaming as if it held its own light.

"What is it?" he whispered.

In The Shadow of Perfection

Mrs. Hartley knelt beside him. Her reflection bloomed in the glass. But it wasn't quite hers. This version was softer, glowing, flawless.

"It's... beautiful," she murmured, fingertips grazing the edge.

The mirror shimmered and, as if answering her touch, spoke.

"You are beautiful inside and out."

Henry gasped, eyes wide. "It talks! Mom, do you think it's magic?" His reflection copied him, only better, tidier, brighter, perfect.

"Not magic," Mrs. Hartley said, though her voice sounded far away. "It's honest."

The mirror's voice came again, lower this time. "Hello, I am Shiny. Henry, you are a beacon of courage. The future shines brightly for you."

Henry puffed out his chest, beaming. "See, Mom? Shiny knows us!"

Mrs. Hartley smiled faintly, but a flicker of unease shadowed her eyes.

Across Edenvale, doors opened, ribbons were untied, and the town awakened to Shiny. The mirrors shimmered on mantels and windowsills, their reflective surfaces quickly becoming the center of conversation.

In her studio, Iris stared at the mirror on her workbench. Shiny sat untouched, yet its presence pressed into the room, stealing the comfort her studio usually gave.

She'd tried to paint that morning. The brush faltered. Every stroke felt hesitant, wrong.

"What troubles you, Iris?" The voice sliced through the silence.

Her hand jerked. Paint splattered across the canvas. She spun, heart hammering. "I'm not troubled," she snapped.

The glass shimmered faintly. "Truth lives in the imperfections... in your paintings. Find it. Paint it. But be careful. You are being watched."

Iris's chest tightened. She turned back to her canvas, but the vibrant colors now seemed to swirl into something chaotic. The painting wasn't hers anymore. It felt wrong.

By midmorning, Edenvale was restless. Whispers traveled faster than the breeze. Shiny had bewitched the town.

In The Shadow of Perfection

Clusters formed in the square. Voices low. Eyes bright. Each person was desperate to share what their mirror had whispered.

Sofia Grant stood by the fountain, her Shiny nestled in a basket like a newborn. "It told me love surrounds me. That my world is beautiful," she said, her tone almost reverent.

Amanda Parker clutched hers tighter, nodding eagerly. "Mine told me my heart is a priceless treasure." Her eyes brimmed, as though Shiny had touched the deepest part of her.

Iris hovered on the edge, listening. Their mirrors offered comfort. Praise. Belonging. Hers had done the opposite. Its words had unsettled her, a thin needle of fear sliding beneath her skin.

She turned away, walking through the town. Everywhere, the same hum. Excitement. Chatter. Laughter. Shiny was in every voice, every home, every glance. As if the glass had woven itself into Edenvale's pulse.

That afternoon, Iris carried a framed canvas to the Parkers' house. They had purchased it at her gallery event, one of many families who insisted her art belonged in their home. Usually, stepping into the

In The Shadow of Perfection

Parkers' kitchen was like being wrapped in a quilt—warm, fragrant with butter and sugar. But today, the air bit with a chill she couldn't explain.

On the mantel, their Shiny glowed. Its light crawled over the walls, filling the room with a shimmer that felt alive. Little Clara twirled before it, her giggles ringing like chimes. "It told her she danced like the wind," Amanda said, smiling at her daughter's delight.

Iris forced a smile, though her throat tightened. The mirror's glow dominated the room, heavy and suffocating. She excused herself quickly, stepping into the late-afternoon air.

Walking home, Iris didn't know whether it was the chill of the breeze or the darkness creeping into her thoughts, but she wrapped her arms around herself, trying to keep warm. She found herself craving a jacket, a cup of tea, something ordinary and comforting. She hurried home.

Back in her studio, Shiny was waiting. It shimmered on the windowsill, drinking in the last thread of daylight.

Her unfinished canvas, the town square at dusk, stared accusingly from the easel. The brush hung loose in her fingers, heavy, useless. And still the mirror glowed, as if it had been waiting for her alone.

In The Shadow of Perfection

"What am I missing?" she whispered to herself, her eyes locked on the painting.

The answer came at once, low and silken.
"You are afraid."

Her head snapped up. "What?" The word shot out, brittle. "Afraid of what?"

The glass rippled, mocking her with its calm.
"Of what lies beneath."

A tremor ran through her hand. Iris set the brush down, crossing the room to perch on the edge of her bed. She dragged Shiny closer, setting it on the nightstand. Its faint glow spilled across the walls, stretching into ghostlike shapes that seemed to hold the room in suspense.

Hesitant, she reached out. Her fingertips brushed the cold frame. The surface quivered like water, and for a heartbeat her reflection wasn't hers. Its head tilted when she didn't move. Its gaze fixed harder, sharper. Watching her.

"You need to look deeper," Shiny murmured. The voice was different now. It was gentler, but edged with warning.

"Look deeper at what?" Her throat was dry.

In The Shadow of Perfection

"Truth hides in the shadows," it breathed. "But not all shadows are safe. Someone is watching you."

Her pulse quickened. A prickling chill spread across her arms. She turned to the corners of the room, her eyes chasing shapes that weren't there.
"Who?" The word cracked in her throat.

The mirror rippled again, warping the glass until her reflection blurred.
"The one who keeps you blind. The one who smiles... and sees everything."

The image that flickered through her mind was swift, ungraspable. A face she knew but couldn't place.

"I don't understand." Her voice fractured, too small against the weight of the moment. "Why are you telling me this? What do you want?"

"I am here to guide you."

The words lingered, heavy and cryptic. Iris pressed her palms to her temples, thoughts spinning. A flicker of memory rose. She heard her own voice, speaking of building a bridge for those who had lost their way. The image hovered, fragile, then slipped from her grasp before she could hold onto it.

In The Shadow of Perfection

"What was that? What should I do?" She broke into tears.

"You must remember! Search your memories. Find the truth," Shiny urged. "But beware. Truth has a price. They are always watching."

Her chest tightened. "Who?"

The glow dimmed, the glass trembling one last time. "Find the shadows within the light. But trust no one... yet."

The silence afterward was louder than words. Iris stared at herself in the glass, though she wasn't sure it was truly her staring back. The room grew colder, shadows unfurling across the walls like black veins creeping closer.

Iris tried to look away, but the mirror's glow held her. In the reflection, a shadow loomed at her shoulder, still and silent. She spun around. The room was empty.

Chapter Five

Rain was rare in Edenvale. That evening, it tapped gently against the windows, soft and steady, as if reminding the town it still existed. Inside Iris's home, the sound only deepened the sense of warmth.

She had spent the afternoon preparing. Delicate china plates and crystal glasses were laid out with care. The table held neat rows of cucumber sandwiches, puff pastries baked to a golden shine, and a bright scatter of macarons. At the center, a pitcher of sparkling punch caught the light, slices of citrus and sprigs of mint floating like decoration.

In the living room, the fire crackled softly, its glow pushing against the shadows, holding the house in a careful cocoon of comfort.

At exactly seven, the doorbell rang. Iris, in a flowing floral dress, opened the door with a warm smile.

Sofia, Rebecca, Amanda, and Mrs. Hartley swept inside together, laughter spilling as they shook off the rain and slipped out of their coats. Their dresses were elegant, hair styled to perfection, eyes bright with the promise of an easy, carefree evening.

"Your home is always so lovely, Iris," Sofia said, handing her a neat bouquet of lilies. "And it smells divine in here."

Iris blushed, setting the flowers in a vase. "Thank you, Sofia. I'm glad you're all here. I thought we could use a little break from routine."

"Indeed!" Amanda laughed, already eyeing the delicate trays on the table. "And it looks like you've outdone yourself again."

They moved into the living room, glasses in hand, settling easily into the rhythm of old friends.

The talk began with families. Rebecca, the youngest, glowed as she spoke. "George surprised me with a weekend away for our tenth anniversary. Just the two of us. It was... perfect."

Mrs. Hartley sighed. "Richard and I barely have a moment with the twins. I don't know how you manage it."

In The Shadow of Perfection

Rebecca's smile didn't falter. "Oh, you know. Everything just falls into place. The children are wonderful. And George, he's always so helpful."

Sofia adjusted her bracelet, leaning forward. "My husband's been in the garden all week. Planting peonies, roses, lavender. Somehow he knows exactly what I want before I even ask."

Iris nodded, keeping her smile in place, topping up glasses, passing around plates. But a familiar pang pulled at her. No husband. No children. No stories to fold neatly into theirs. She listened instead, smoothing the edges of the evening, while something hollow pressed harder against her chest.

The conversation turned to their children, stories flowing easily. Mrs. Hartley spoke about her daughter's recital, every note flawless, the whole hall applauding. Amanda followed with details of a family picnic where nothing had gone wrong, not even the weather. "It was just right," she said with a satisfied smile.

Eventually, the talk shifted to Shiny. The women's eyes lit up, voices quickening as they compared notes, each eager to share how the mirrors had slipped into their daily lives.

In The Shadow of Perfection

"Shiny told me my dress was perfect this morning," Amanda said, her face glowing. "And you know what? I actually felt... beautiful. More than I have in years."

"Not strange at all," Rebecca laughed. "I feel it too. It's as if Shiny only ever sees the best in us."

Sofia leaned forward, her expression bright. "Mine always tells me I light up a room the moment I walk in. It sounds silly, but it gives me such confidence, like it sees something I can't."

Mrs. Hartley gave a slow, contented smile. "We are blessed, aren't we? Everything in our lives is so beautiful. Of course, Shiny sees it too."

Iris listened, sipping her punch. She wanted to share their enthusiasm, to bask in the same happiness, but she couldn't shake the unease that had been growing inside her. Clearing her throat, she set down her glass.

"I'm glad Shiny makes you all feel that way," she said carefully. "But... have any of you noticed anything odd about your Shiny?"

The women paused, exchanging puzzled glances. Amanda furrowed her brow. "Odd? In what way, Iris?"

"Well," Iris began, choosing her words with caution, "sometimes mine goes silent. It doesn't always respond to me like it should. And I've noticed little things, small imperfections, things I never saw before."

There was a brief, uncomfortable silence before Sofia spoke up, her tone gentle but confused. "Imperfections? What kind of imperfections?"

"Like... a picture frame that isn't straight or a flower that doesn't bloom quite right," Iris said, feeling foolish as she heard the words aloud. "And Shiny doesn't always reassure me like it used to. It's strange, but it feels like it's... different."

Amanda laughed lightly, shaking her head. "Oh, Iris, you're being silly. Everything is perfect, and Shiny only shows us what's true. Let's have a look at yours."

Before Iris could protest, the women were on their feet, heading toward the living room where her Shiny hung above the fireplace. They crowded around, examining the mirror with curious eyes, waiting for it to speak.

"Shiny," Sofia said brightly, stepping closer, "don't you think we look lovely tonight?"

Shiny's glass shimmered in the firelight, and its melodic voice filled the room. "You are radiant, Sofia," it said. "All of you are beautiful and perfect, just as always."

In The Shadow of Perfection

The women beamed, glancing at each other with satisfied smiles, while Iris stood apart, feeling a chill settle over her. Shiny's words were kind, but they rang hollow in her ears. She forced herself to smile, hiding her disappointment as the women returned to their seats, chattering happily about Shiny's latest compliments.

As the conversation moved on, Iris took a deep breath, determined to share her deeper concerns. "Would you all... come with me to my studio?" she asked, her voice quieter now. "There's something I want to show you."

Intrigued, the women followed her down the hall, their voices low, echoing against the walls. Iris pushed open the door to her studio. Easels and canvases filled the space, the kind of organized chaos only an artist could understand. The air smelled of turpentine and fresh paint, a scent that had always grounded her.

She gestured toward the canvases stacked against the far wall, covered by a sheet. "These are my latest," she said, her voice unsteady. "But something's wrong. I can't paint the way I used to. Everything looks different now... and I thought you should see."

Her hand trembled as she tugged the sheet aside.

The women leaned forward, waiting.

In The Shadow of Perfection

Blank.

Every canvas stood untouched, white and empty, as though she had never lifted a brush.

A chorus of gasps filled the room. Confusion rippled across their faces.

"But... Iris, there's nothing here," Mrs. Hartley said at last, her brow furrowing. "You told us you'd been working on these for weeks."

"I have," Iris whispered, her voice so faint it barely carried. "I painted them. I swear I did. I don't understand..."

Sofia's smile faltered. She reached out, fingertips brushing one of the blank canvases as though the paint might rise to meet her. "Maybe you've pushed yourself too hard," she said softly. "The exhibition, the festival. It's no wonder you're worn out."

Amanda folded her arms, taking a step back. "Yes, it's just stress. Everything is still perfect, Iris. Maybe you just need a break."

"I don't know..." Iris's eyes flicked from canvas to canvas, then back to the faces around her. "It feels like I'm losing something. Like the perfection I used to see... it isn't there anymore."

In The Shadow of Perfection

Rebecca placed a firm hand on her shoulder, her voice steady. "Iris, look around! Look at your home, your life. It's perfect. Maybe all you are experiencing now is just a phase, or maybe it's stress."

The women exchanged glances, uneasy but unwilling to linger in the discomfort. One by one, they drifted back toward the living room, their reassurances smoothing over Iris's words. Iris lingered at the studio door, staring at the blank canvases. For the first time, she wondered if she'd ever painted them at all.

Her friends' laughter floated back through the hall, warm and practiced. Soon, the conversation returned to safe ground. They talked about family, schedules, the ease of perfect lives. But in the silence of her studio, Iris could swear she heard something else, a faint whisper rising from the empty canvases.

Chapter Six

After Iris's guests had left, her sense of isolation had only deepened. She closed the door, turning back to her quiet home, and made her way to the living room. Shiny hung silently over the fireplace, the room dark and shadowed now that the fire had burned low. She walked to the mirror, feeling a strange compulsion to speak.

"Shiny," she said, her voice trembling, "why don't they understand?"

The mirror's surface seemed to ripple, and its voice, cool and calm, filled the air. "They cannot see what you see, Iris. Their world is flawless, and they have no need for doubt."

Tears pricked at the corners of her eyes. "But... What about me? Why do I feel this way?"

"Because you are different," Shiny replied, its tone soft but unyielding. "You see beyond the surface, and that frightens them. They will never understand."

In The Shadow of Perfection

Iris took a shaky step back, her pulse quickening as she stared at Shiny's flawless surface. There was no comfort in its reflection, only a detached truth that made her blood run cold. She backed away until her legs hit the edge of the sofa, and she sank down heavily, her breathing shallow.

"Why can't I paint anymore?" she asked, her voice breaking. "What's happening to me?"

Shiny remained silent for a long moment, and she thought for a fleeting second that it wouldn't answer. Then it spoke, its tone taking on a strange, almost mocking lilt. "Perhaps, deep down inside, you are starting to remember. Perhaps your eyes have been opened to what has always been there."

She shuddered, her hands gripping the sofa's edge as if it were the only thing keeping her grounded. "Remember what? I don't want to feel this way. I was happy. I loved my work; I loved my life. Everything was beautiful."

"Was it?" Shiny replied, the question hanging in the air like a shadow. "Or were you simply painting over the cracks, pretending they didn't exist? You are not like the others, Iris. You were never like them."

Iris's breath hitched, a desperate sob escaping her lips. She felt like she was drowning, the weight of those words pulling her down. For the first time, she couldn't find the familiar comfort of perfection that had always been her sanctuary. The flaws she had tried so hard to ignore now seemed to glare back at her from every corner of the room.

"No," she whispered, shaking her head, tears streaming down her face. "I don't want this. I want everything to be perfect again."

"Perfection is an illusion," Shiny said, its voice growing darker, almost predatory. "You have been pretending you were happy for too long. You are beginning to see what lies beneath, and you will never unsee it."

"Stop it!" she cried, her voice hoarse and raw. "Stop talking to me!"

But Shiny did not stop. Its voice softened, almost coaxing, like a parent speaking to a frightened child. "You don't have to be afraid, Iris. I will show you the truth, even if they cannot see it. You are not alone."

A scream of frustration bubbled up inside her, and she grabbed the nearest object, a delicate porcelain vase from the side table. With a surge of fury, she hurled it at Shiny. The vase shattered against the wall beside the mirror, pieces scattering across the floor, but Shiny remained unscathed, its glass reflecting her rage with an almost taunting calm.

Exhausted and broken, she stumbled away from the living room and up the stairs to her bedroom, each step feeling heavier than the last. The air seemed thicker, as if the house itself had become a cage, suffocating her with its oppressive stillness. She reached her bedroom, slamming the door behind her, her breath coming in ragged gasps.

She sank to the floor, curling up against the bed frame, her knees drawn tightly to her chest. Her eyes burned with unshed tears, and the darkness in the room pressed in, suffocating. She squeezed her eyes shut, praying for sleep to take her away from this nightmare, for everything to be normal when she woke up.

Hours passed, or maybe minutes. Time seemed to blur. Her body grew cold, and she barely noticed the tears drying on her cheeks. She felt a crushing weight on her chest, a desperate need to escape, but there was nowhere to go, nowhere to hide.

Then, just as she began to drift into a restless and fitful sleep, she heard a soft voice—barely more than a breath, filling the darkness like a secret.

"I will be here, Iris. Always."

In The Shadow of Perfection

Her eyes flew open, but the room was empty, bathed only in the pale moonlight that slipped through the curtains. She turned toward the door, half-expecting to see a shadow, but there was nothing, only the silence of her empty house, and the echo of the words she could not escape.

She lay awake until the first light of dawn, unable to move, paralyzed by the fear that the world she had loved was no longer hers to understand. And for the first time in her life, she felt truly alone. She was trapped in a reality where perfection had shattered, leaving only the fragments of a truth she was too afraid to face.

The silence in her room wasn't calming; it was suffocating. Even the soft tapping of tree branches against the window sounded deliberate, as though something outside was trying to get in.

Then it came, the softest creak of a floorboard downstairs.

Iris froze, her breath caught in her throat. She strained her ears, her pulse pounding in her skull, trying to convince herself it was nothing. The house always made sounds, didn't it? Old houses did that. That's all it was.

Another creak, louder this time.

In The Shadow of Perfection

Her heart raced. She sat up, moving slowly, her eyes fixed on the closed bedroom door as if expecting it to burst open. A new sound followed, a faint scrape, like something being dragged across the wooden floors below.

"Shiny," she whispered into the dark, though she knew the mirror couldn't hear her. "What's happening?"

The silence stretched thick and heavy. And then from the downstairs living room, she heard it.

A voice.

It wasn't clear enough to make out all the words, but it sounded like someone having a hushed conversation. She slid out of bed, her bare feet sinking into the cold floor, the air around her growing colder still.

"You need to reprogram it." She heard a male voice.

She could hear it. It was the unmistakable murmur of words not meant for her ears. "Sleeping... trying to remember... destroy Edenvale."

Trembling, she moved toward the door and pressed her ear against the wood. The voice faded to a whisper, and for a moment, there was nothing but her own ragged breathing. Then, faintly: "Can't let it happen. She could ruin everything."

In The Shadow of Perfection

She jerked back from the door, her hand flying to her mouth to stifle the scream rising in her throat. Her heart hammered against her ribs, and tears pricked her eyes as she backed away from the door, her body trembling uncontrollably. She stumbled back, knocking into her nightstand, sending a framed photograph crashing to the floor. The sound splintered the silence, but it was quickly swallowed by the oppressive stillness that followed. The whispers were gone.

Her gaze darted to the window. Outside, dawn bled slowly across the horizon, pale and thin, but it didn't soften the shadows pressing against the glass. They seemed to lean closer, waiting.

Shiny had been right.

Someone was watching her.

And this time, she was sure they were inside the house.

Chapter Seven

Iris sat motionless in front of her latest canvas. The air in the studio felt dense, oppressive, as though the room itself had decided to smother her creativity. Her brush hovered over the canvas, trembling, a bead of black paint threatening to drop onto the warped depiction of Edenvale she had been struggling with for days. The moment the bristles touched the canvas, the yellow curdled into a sickly green, spreading across the dark streaks like a disease.

"No!" Iris dropped the brush, the clatter unnaturally loud in the suffocating silence.

Her heart pounded as her gaze darted to the other canvases scattered across the room. Each told a similar story. Edenvale had become twisted and unrecognizable. The river, once shimmering like glass, now ran black as oil. The fountain, typically the heart of the town, stood cracked and dry, its stone figures warped and grotesque.

In The Shadow of Perfection

"What's happening to me?" she whispered, her voice cracking. She pressed a paint-streaked hand to her forehead, but no answers came.

Her reflection in Shiny caught her eye. It shimmered faintly from its spot on the windowsill, as if mocking her despair. She walked toward it, unable to tear her gaze from the glass. Her own face stared back at her, but it wasn't quite right. Her eyes, once full of life, were bloodshot and ringed with shadows. Her skin looked paper-thin, and her hollow cheeks gave her the appearance of someone being consumed from the inside out. She needed to get out.

By late afternoon, Iris was drifting through Edenvale's streets. The sun sat low, casting long beams of gold across the town like a spotlight on a stage.

People passed her with easy smiles, their voices light, their steps unhurried. On the surface, everything was as it should be.

And yet... their movements jarred her. Too smooth. Too practiced. As if each smile, each laugh, had been rehearsed and performed on cue.

She stopped outside the bakery. The display, normally piled high with bread and pastries, was bare. Curtains were drawn tight behind the glass.

In The Shadow of Perfection

She couldn't shake the feeling she wasn't alone. Something watched from the other side.

She turned toward the square, her steps slowing. The fountain rose at the center, cobblestones around it gleaming as though freshly polished. The water caught the last of the sunlight, sparkling bright, yet it looked lifeless. Wrong.

Something shifted.

A shadow bled across the base of the fountain, darker than the light allowed. Iris froze, heart pounding. For a second, she was certain someone was there. Perhaps a figure, half-hidden in the dark.

She blinked. The shadow thinned. The figure was gone.

By the time Iris reached home, her chest was tight with unease. She shut the door quickly behind her, twisting the lock with shaking fingers before retreating to the studio.

Canvases leaned against every wall—unfinished, distorted, wrong. The Edenvale she once painted with ease no longer existed in her work. What stared back at her now was lifeless, brittle. Shadows bled across the colors, shifting when she wasn't looking.

A knock broke the silence. Soft. Deliberate.

In The Shadow of Perfection

Iris froze, her breath catching in her throat.

"Iris?" Sofia's voice called from the other side of the door. "It's me. Let me in."

Iris hesitated, then shuffled to the door, her hand trembling as she turned the knob. Sofia stepped inside, her warm smile faltering as she took in Iris's disheveled appearance and the chaos of the studio.

"I was worried about you," Sofia said, setting a small bag on the cluttered coffee table. "You haven't been answering your phone."

"I've been busy," Iris muttered, avoiding her gaze.

Sofia glanced around the room, her brow furrowing. "This doesn't look like busy. It looks like you've been going through something. I want to help you."

"I'm fine," Iris said quickly, crossing her arms. "What's that?" She nodded toward the bag.

"Dr. Reynolds asked me to bring it over," Sofia said, her tone careful. "He said it's something to help with... whatever you're going through. He's worried about you, Iris. We all are."

Iris's stomach twisted as she stared at the bag. "Medicine?"

In The Shadow of Perfection

Sofia nodded. "He said it'll help you sleep, help you... feel better."

Iris's pulse quickened, her unease deepening. "I don't need it."

Sofia reached for her hand, her expression softening. "Iris, please. Just try it. You haven't been yourself lately."

Iris didn't reply. She grabbed the bag and shoved it into a drawer, her hands trembling. "Thanks for bringing it over, but I'll be fine."

Sofia hesitated, then nodded. "If you're sure..."

"I am," Iris said, her tone firm. "Thanks for stopping by."

Sofia lingered, her concern evident, but she eventually left, leaving Iris alone with the oppressive silence.

The moment the door clicked shut, Shiny spoke firmly. "Do not take it! It is not meant to help you."

Iris sat heavily on the sofa, her head in her hands. "What's happening to me? Why is everything falling apart?"

"Because you are beginning to see," Shiny replied, its tone calm but urgent. "The cracks in the illusion. The truth hidden beneath."

"What truth?" Iris whispered, her voice cracking.

In The Shadow of Perfection

Shiny shimmered, its surface rippling like liquid. "This place is not what it seems. You must leave. Tonight."

Iris's breath hitched. "Leave? Where would I go? There's nowhere to go."

"There is a way," Shiny said. "A path beyond the mountain. But you must act quickly. They are watching you."

Iris's heart raced as she stared at the mirror. "Who's watching me?"

Shiny didn't answer. Instead, its surface darkened, revealing a faint, flickering image, a map. The winding trails of Edenvale's outskirts were faintly outlined, and at the edge, a small opening glowed faintly.

"What is that?" Iris asked, leaning closer.

"Your escape," Shiny replied. "Follow the path. Do not stop. Do not turn back."

Iris's hands clenched into fists, her mind a whirlwind of fear and determination. "I can't just leave. What about my friends? What about Sofia?"

"If you stay, you will lose yourself," Shiny said, its voice almost pleading. "The truth is waiting, but you cannot find it here."

In The Shadow of Perfection

Iris's breath came in shallow gasps as she stood, her resolve hardening. She grabbed her coat and keys, her movements jerky and frantic. Her gaze lingered on Shiny for a moment, a mix of gratitude and dread swirling in her chest.

"Thank you," she whispered, though she wasn't sure why.

Shiny shimmered faintly, its final words soft but insistent. "Remember, Iris. Trust what you see. Trust your memories."

With that, she stormed out into the night, the cold air biting at her skin as she climbed into her car. Her hands trembled on the steering wheel, but her grip tightened as she started the engine. She glanced in the rearview mirror, half-expecting to see someone or something following her.

The streets of Edenvale were eerily quiet as she drove through the town, the perfect houses and glowing windows feeling more like a trap than a home. She didn't look back. She couldn't. But in the rearview mirror, a figure stood in the middle of the road, motionless, watching her taillights disappear.

Chapter Eight

The car roared to life, headlights carving through the dark. Iris gripped the wheel so tightly her hands ached, her knuckles bone-white. She pressed harder on the accelerator.

Edenvale blurred past her windows. Rows of perfect houses, manicured lawns, the same tidy streets she'd walked a thousand times. Tonight, they looked unreal. Stage scenery flashing by, ready to collapse if she looked too closely.

Her thoughts tangled, fragments colliding with no clear thread. She was running, but from what and to where? It didn't matter. She only knew she had to get out. To reach the edge of Edenvale. To prove there was one.

Her voice cracked the silence inside the car. "Why do I feel like this?" she whispered to herself, gripping the wheel harder. "Why can't I remember anything?"

Flashes of memories or dreams, perhaps? They began to surface, vivid and fleeting. She saw a small boy with curly hair, his laughter ringing in her ears. A man's warm, steady hand resting on her shoulder. A house that wasn't in Edenvale, its front porch bathed in golden evening light. But as quickly as they appeared, they vanished, leaving only confusion in their wake.

The road stretched endlessly before her, and she pressed harder on the accelerator, the speedometer climbing. The wind howled outside the car, the world beyond the windshield a swirling blur of shadows and faint glimmers of light.

"I don't belong here," she whispered, her voice cracking. "I've never belonged here."

The flashbacks came again, this time sharper, more insistent. She saw herself in a white coat, standing in a bright, sterile room. Charts and notes cluttered her desk. Faces swam before her, a young couple holding hands, their expressions hopeful yet weary.

"Dr. Valen, what do you think?" A voice came from nowhere. It was familiar, yet impossibly far away.

In the haze of memory, she turned. Her own voice answered, steady and certain, though it no longer felt like hers. "I think we can help them. We have to."

The vision dissolved, replaced by the sound of children's laughter. Two small figures ran across a sunlit field, their giggles echoing in her ears. "Mama, come catch us!" one called, his voice sweet and full of joy. She saw herself reaching out to them, but before she could touch them, the image shattered like glass, leaving her gasping for breath.

The road began to curve, but Iris barely noticed. Her mind was a cacophony of fragmented memories and desperate questions. She thought of Sofia's words, so casual, so oblivious. "Maybe you just need some sleep, Iris."

She gritted her teeth, her hands gripping the wheel tighter. "It's not just sleep," she hissed. "It's this place, it's all of this."

The trees leaned closer, branches twisting into hooked fingers. Streetlights flickered, throwing long, broken shadows across the lane. She blinked rapidly, her vision blurring with tears.

"Why can't I remember?" she cried, her voice breaking. "Who am I? Where did I come from?"

Shiny's voice echoed in her mind, a haunting melody that refused to be silenced. "You were placed here, Iris. You don't belong."

The words sent a shiver down her spine. She shook her head violently, as if she could dislodge the voice from her thoughts. "No," she whispered. "That's not true. It can't be true."

The memories surged again, sharper this time. She saw herself in the driver seat of another car, her hands gripping the steering wheel, much like now. But the scene was different. Bright sunlight streamed through the windows, and the laughter of children filled the air. She glanced in the rearview mirror and saw two small, beautiful faces, smiling and carefree.

Then a flash of blinding light. The deafening screech of tires. The sickening crunch of metal.

The memory slammed into her like a physical blow, and she gasped, her vision swimming. Her car swerved as she lost focus, the tires skidding on the wet pavement.

"No..." The word broke out of her in a sob. Tears streamed down her face. "That's not me. That's not my life."

But some part of her knew it was. The memories belonged to her. They always had.

The car veered again. Out of nowhere, a deer froze in the headlights, its eyes glowing wide but hollow. Iris's hands wrenched the wheel. The car spun out of control, the tires screeching against the asphalt. She felt the world tilt, the trees and road blending into a chaotic blur.

In The Shadow of Perfection

Time seemed to stretch. The vehicle collided with a tree. The impact jarred her teeth and sent a searing ache down her spine. The airbag punched into her chest, pain exploding through her ribs. The sound of breaking glass filled her ears. And then... Silence.

She sat slumped against the seat, her head pounding, blood trickling down her temple. The smell of smoke and gasoline filled the air, mingling with the metallic tang of blood. She tried to move, but her body protested, every muscle screaming in pain.

Through the shattered windshield, she saw the trees swaying in the night breeze, their branches clawing at the sky like desperate hands. Somewhere in the distance, a faint, rhythmic glow pulsed in the darkness, growing brighter with each beat.

Her vision blurred, and the world began to fade. But just before the darkness claimed her, she heard it. Shiny's voice, soft and insidious, whispering from the depths of her mind.

"You can't run, Iris. The truth will always find you."

And then there was nothing.

Chapter Nine

Iris drifted in and out of consciousness, reality splintering into hard edges of pain. The steering wheel bit into her ribs; every shallow breath flared heat through her chest. The air burned—chemical sting at the back of her throat mixed with the metallic taste of blood. She couldn't tell if the sound ringing in her ears was the distant echo of the crash or the pounding of her heart.

Somewhere between the sharp sting of pain and the suffocating weight of the darkness, memories began to surface, not as a comforting balm but as disjointed flashes that made no sense.

The sunlight dappled through a canopy of leaves, and Iris sat cross-legged on a picnic blanket. A child's laughter filled the air, a sweet, lilting sound that tugged at her heart. She turned her head, and there they were—a boy with curls the color of caramel, chasing a girl clutching a stuffed rabbit. They circled her, giggling; the stuffed rabbit dragged a dusty ear through the grass.

In The Shadow of Perfection

"Careful, you two!" she called, her tone tinged with warmth and an edge of caution.

Strong arms slid around her waist from behind, and she felt herself lean back into the embrace. A man's voice murmured in her ear, low and soothing. "They're happy. Let them be."

She turned to see his face, but the memory flickered and dissolved, leaving her grasping at the edges of something she couldn't quite hold.

Her eyes fluttered open to the dark, chaotic reality of the crash. Glass glittered like frost on the dashboard. She tried to move, but her body screamed in rebellion.

The seatbelt cut deep into her shoulder. She lifted a trembling hand to release it and saw her fingers smeared with blood and dirt.

Her breaths came short and jagged. She was drowning. The car wasn't a vehicle anymore; it was a cage. Panic clawed at her as she fumbled for the door handle. At last, it gave.

The door groaned open, and the night air rushed in, icy against her skin.

Iris collapsed onto the soaked ground. Cold seeped into her clothes, mud clinging to her feet. The world tilted, spinning, her vision breaking into fragments. Somewhere in the distance, a faint light beckoned, wavering like a mirage.

And then Shiny's voice came. Soft. Invasive. Impossible. "You're beginning to see, Iris. Keep going."

Her head jerked up, her pulse quickening despite her exhaustion. "Why are you doing this to me?" she croaked, her voice raw and broken. "What is happening to me?"

"Answers come at a cost," Shiny replied, its tone calm yet loaded with a weight she couldn't decipher. "You must be willing to face them."

Another memory slammed into her, sharp and relentless.

A lecture hall. Bright overhead lights hummed softly as rows of students sat at attention, their notebooks open, pens poised to capture every word. Iris stood at the front, wearing a tailored suit, her hair swept into a professional updo. A diagram of the human brain illuminated the projector screen behind her.

"The limbic system," she said, her voice measured and confident, "is responsible for our emotional lives. Fear, joy, love—they all stem from this complex network of structures."

In The Shadow of Perfection

Her laser pointer swept across the image, pausing on the amygdala. "This small, almond-shaped region is particularly fascinating. It's the trigger for our fight-or-flight response. The question I want you to consider is: what happens when this response becomes perpetual? When fear takes hold and never lets go?"

Her audience scribbled furiously, hanging on her every word. But as Iris turned back to the diagram, the screen began to flicker. The brain image warped. The amygdala ballooned, swallowing the cortex; the projector buzzed loudly, and the room grew darker.

She turned to the students, but their faces were gone, replaced by featureless masks. A wave of nausea swept over her, and the memory dissolved into the cold, suffocating reality of the crash.

Iris groaned, pressing her hands to her temples as if she could force the memories to make sense. The pain in her head throbbed in rhythm with her heartbeat, her body trembling as she tried to pull herself to her feet.

She stumbled forward, each step unsteady, the ground beneath her seeming to shift. Her thoughts spiraled, flashes of her past colliding with the stark, unbearable reality of Edenvale.

In The Shadow of Perfection

Nothing fit. Nothing made sense. How had she come to this place? Who had she been before?

"Keep going," Shiny whispered again, its voice coming from her own mind now. "You're closer than you think."

Her breath hitched as another memory struck her with the force of a physical blow.

The soft hum of a research lab surrounded her. Iris stood at the head of a round table, its polished surface reflecting the glowing screen behind her. The screen displayed a series of graphs and charts, their lines rising and falling in intricate patterns. Words like *Hedonic Adaptation* and *Sustainable Euphoria Index* were scrawled across the headers in bold type.

"Happiness is not just an emotion," Iris said, her voice steady, authoritative. "It's a state of being that can be cultivated, studied, and if we're precise enough, engineered."

The small group of colleagues nodded, their faces a mix of intrigue and skepticism.

"And the Eden Project?" someone asked, their tone laced with curiosity.

Iris glanced at the documents in her hands. "A controlled environment. A perfect community where every factor contributing to human happiness is optimized. If we can measure what makes people truly happy, we can create a blueprint, a universal formula for joy."

"But at what cost?" another colleague interjected, their brow furrowed. "Can happiness be sustainable if it's artificial? If they realize it's... not real?"

"Real or not, happiness is still happiness," Iris replied sharply, her tone brooking no argument. "If we can engineer sustainable happiness, we have a duty to try."

The room faded into darkness, the memory slipping through her fingers like sand.

Iris stumbled to her knees, her body wracked with sobs. The fragments of memories were cutting into her like shards of broken glass. Her mind reeled, struggling to reconcile the life she had glimpsed with the suffocating perfection of Edenvale.

"This isn't real," she whispered, her voice shaking. "None of this is real."

"Now you're starting to understand," she imagined Shiny would say with an approving tone.

The light ahead grew brighter, flickering like a beacon in the darkness. Iris forced herself to stand, her legs unsteady as she staggered forward. She didn't know where she was going or what she would find, but she couldn't stay here. She had to escape. She needed to find answers, to piece together the truth.

The ground beneath her feet was uneven, her vision blurring as exhaustion and pain clouded her senses. She closed her eyes, hoping to wipe away the excruciating pain.

Somewhere, far off, a siren cut the night—thin at first, then rising, slicing through Edenvale like a blade. Ahead, the light flickered... closer than before.

Chapter Ten

The morning after the crash dawned with an unsettling quiet over Edenvale. The sky held a polite, powdered gray, as if the day itself didn't want to be noticed. Whispers spread quickly among the townsfolk, drawing small groups to the neat cobblestone streets and pristine porches. The air buzzed with a blend of curiosity and disbelief.

"Did you hear about Iris?" Mrs. Haverly's voice, usually melodic and soothing, carried a tremor as she spoke to her neighbor, Mr. Bernard, over the white picket fence that separated their immaculate yards.

Mr. Bernard adjusted his glasses, his expression both skeptical and concerned. "A car crash," he murmured. "In Edenvale? It's... unheard of."

"No one loses control here. Not unless they mean to," Mrs. Haverly said, shaking her head. Her neatly styled hair gleamed in the morning light.

In The Shadow of Perfection

Across the street, Sofia stood on her porch, her arms crossed. She listened to the murmurs but didn't join in. Something about the way people spoke of Iris made her uneasy. Their words were tinged with pity, confusion, and an undercurrent of judgment that didn't sit right with her.

"She's always been... different." Diana's voice floated from a nearby cluster of neighbors. "You know how artists are. Maybe she was having one of those... episodes."

Sofia's jaw tightened. "Episodes," she muttered under her breath, annoyed by the dismissive tone. Iris wasn't some fragile thing to be dissected over morning tea. She was her friend, and now she was lying in a hospital bed, and no one seemed to care enough to understand why.

"Her paintings," Rebecca added in a hushed voice, joining the group. "Have you seen them lately? They've been... dark. Not at all like her usual work. Maybe it's a sign she's been... losing herself."

"I've heard rumors that she's been shutting herself in that studio of hers for days at a time," Mrs. Haverly said, lowering her voice conspiratorially. "What if... what if she's been hiding something?"

In The Shadow of Perfection

"Hiding what?" Mr. Bernard asked, frowning. "That's ridiculous. Iris is a beloved part of this community. She's just… struggling."

But the whispers didn't stop. "Struggling or not," Diana said, "this crash is more than an accident. It's a sign."

Sofia clenched her fists, her frustration mounting. She turned and went back inside her house, slamming the door behind her. The echo of their words stayed with her, gnawing at her thoughts. Was it true? Had she missed something? Sofia thought of Iris's recent behavior—the withdrawn silences, the haunted look in her eyes. And yet, none of it felt like enough to explain this.

The Edenvale Medical Center rose in the middle of town, gleaming like a jewel of glass and steel. Its sleek facade mirrored the perfect streets and manicured greenery around it, every reflection as flawless as the world it served. A row of clipped hedges lined the path to the entrance, and at its center, a marble angel smiled down from a fountain, water bubbling at her feet as if nothing bad could ever happen here.

Inside, the perfection only deepened. White floors shone under recessed lighting, not a mark or scuff in sight. Pastel paintings lined the walls—soft waves, bright meadows, endless blue skies. The art was carefully selected to keep visitors calm. Even the air smelled faintly of lavender, a fragrance designed to soothe.

But beneath the polish lay something else. No phones ringing. No voices. No footsteps. A single monitor beeped somewhere far off, then stopped—as if it remembered it wasn't needed here. The silence pressed against the walls, the building immaculate yet hollow, like a stage set waiting for actors who never arrived.

Edenvale Medical Center wasn't a place of healing. It was a showpiece. A promise carved in glass and steel that no one in this town would ever need saving. People didn't fall ill here. They didn't suffer. The hospital stood more as comfort than cure, a silent reassurance that perfection was permanent.

But today, perfection had cracked. Something had gone wrong.

Dr. Reynolds, the hospital's chief physician, stood at the foot of Iris's bed, his face unreadable. His white coat was spotless, his demeanor calm, but there was a flicker of something in his eyes—something he quickly masked as Nurse Louise entered the room.

"Vitals are stabilizing," Nurse Louise reported, her voice tight. She glanced at Iris, her pale face framed by dark hair that clung to her damp skin. "But... she's not waking up. It's almost like... she doesn't want to."

Dr. Reynolds nodded slowly, his gaze lingering on the faint lines of pain etched into Iris's face. "She's holding on," he said quietly. "But just barely."

Louise hesitated. "Sir, I've never seen anything like this. No one... no one gets hurt like this here. What do we... what do we do?"

Dr. Reynolds's expression hardened. "We keep her comfortable. That's all we can do for now."

Louise nodded, though her unease was palpable. She adjusted the IV line with careful precision, her hands trembling slightly. The machines around Iris beeped softly, their rhythmic tones foreign in a hospital where equipment was more ornamental than functional.

Outside the hospital, the townspeople lingered, their whispers growing louder.

"Do you think she'll recover?" one woman asked, clutching her pearl necklace as if it were a talisman.

"She has to," another replied, her voice trembling. "What would it mean for the rest of us if she didn't?"

Sofia arrived at the hospital, her steps purposeful despite the weight of uncertainty pressing down on her.

In The Shadow of Perfection

She pushed through the small crowd gathered near the entrance, ignoring the curious glances and murmured questions. Inside, the receptionist greeted her with the practiced smile that seemed to be a requirement in Edenvale.

"I'm here to see Iris," Sofia said firmly.

The receptionist hesitated, her smile faltering for a fraction of a second before she nodded. "Room 204," she said. "But please, keep it brief. She needs rest."

Sofia found Iris's room easily. The door was slightly ajar, and she could see her friend lying still on the bed, her face pale and serene against the soft pillows. Dr. Reynolds stood at the foot of the bed, his posture rigid as he reviewed the monitors.

"Dr. Reynolds," Sofia greeted, her voice steady despite the turmoil in her chest.

He turned, his expression carefully neutral. "Sofia. I wasn't expecting visitors so soon."

"I'm her friend," Sofia said, stepping into the room. "I need to see her."

Dr. Reynolds hesitated, then nodded. "She's stable for now. But she needs rest."

In The Shadow of Perfection

Sofia approached the bed, her gaze softening as she looked at Iris. Her friend's face was pale, framed by dark bruises that marred her otherwise perfect complexion. She reached out, her hand trembling slightly as she touched Iris's cold fingers.

"Iris," she whispered, her voice breaking. "It's me. Sofia. Please... wake up."

Dr. Reynolds watched the interaction silently, his expression unreadable. When Sofia finally turned to face him, her eyes were sharp.

"What happened to her?" she demanded.

Dr. Reynolds hesitated, then sighed. "It's difficult to say. The crash was severe, but her injuries... they're not as extensive as you might expect. It's almost as if... she's fighting something we can't see."

Sofia frowned. "That doesn't make sense."

"None of this does," he admitted, his voice low. "But we're doing everything we can."

Sofia's gaze lingered on him for a moment longer, suspicion flickering in her eyes. Then she turned back to Iris, her heart heavy with worry.

When Sofia left the hospital, the whispers outside grew louder. She ignored them, her thoughts racing as she made her way home. Something about the hospital, about Dr. Reynolds, didn't feel right. The town had always been strange, but now, cracks were beginning to show. And she couldn't shake the feeling that those cracks ran deeper than anyone realized.

As she walked, the perfect streets of Edenvale felt less inviting. The cheerful houses and manicured lawns seemed to watch her, their pristine facades hiding something she couldn't yet name. For the first time, she felt truly alone.

Back at the hospital, Dr. Reynolds stood alone in Iris's room. He glanced at the monitors, then at the woman lying still on the bed. He leaned closer, his voice barely a whisper.

"Iris," he said, his tone soft but firm. "You need to wake up. You're not finished yet."

For a moment, nothing happened. Then Iris's fingers twitched, her breathing hitching as her eyelids fluttered. Dr. Reynolds didn't move. "Good," he murmured. "We're ready to begin."

Chapter Eleven

Sofia replayed her visit to the hospital as she walked home, her steps slow and deliberate. The air in Edenvale was crisp and still, the kind of stillness that seemed to breathe down the neck, pressing its presence against every thought. Despite the perfectly paved streets and manicured lawns, a chill ran through her, one she couldn't shake. She turned down the familiar lane toward her house, but her mind lingered in the stark whiteness of the hospital room, trapped in an uneasy loop.

The hospital had been pristine—too pristine. Sofia had always thought of Edenvale Medical Center as little more than a glorified art gallery: all polished floors and soothing pastel art. It was there as a reassurance, not a necessity. People didn't get hurt here, not like this. Yet seeing Iris lying so still in that oversized bed, connected to machines that beeped and hummed with alien precision, had turned something inside her.

In The Shadow of Perfection

What gnawed at her now, hours later, was how utterly useless those machines had seemed. The monitors' bright lights and fluctuating lines told a story of life, but Iris hadn't moved. Dr. Reynolds had stood nearby, a statue of calm authority, but there was something in his eyes—a flicker too fleeting to be a mistake. Was it uncertainty? Fear?

Sofia shook her head, trying to clear the memory as she approached her own home. Yet it clung to her like cobwebs.

She tried to compare the woman she'd known—her vibrancy, her fire—with the motionless figure lying in that hospital bed. Then she thought of the doctor.

"She's stable," Dr. Reynolds had said, his voice smooth, deliberate.

"Stable," Sofia had repeated flatly. It wasn't a lie, but it didn't feel like the truth either.

Dr. Reynolds stood stiffly, his hands clasped behind his back, his white coat spotless. He was the embodiment of professionalism, yet Sofia couldn't shake the feeling that something about him didn't quite fit. It seemed like he belonged to the hospital, but not to Edenvale.

"Do you know what caused the crash?" she had asked, not breaking her gaze from Iris.

In The Shadow of Perfection

"A loss of control," he'd said. His response was quick and rehearsed.

"She's not reckless," Sofia had pressed. "She wouldn't drive like that. It doesn't make sense."

His expression barely shifted. "Sometimes the mind… strays. Especially when it's burdened."

Sofia's head snapped toward him. "Burdened? By what?"

A flicker of hesitation. Then, smooth again. "Stress. Exhaustion. You know how hard she's been working. Perhaps it's taken its toll."

Sofia narrowed her eyes, the first spark of doubt turning sharp. "Iris hasn't been herself lately, that's true. But this? This isn't stress. There's something else, isn't there? You're not telling me everything."

Dr. Reynolds gave a small smile, the kind meant to soothe but only set her teeth on edge. "Sofia, I understand your concern. But rest assured, we're doing everything for her. What she needs is time."

The conversation had ended there, but the unease remained.

As Sofia made her way down the corridor, every detail pressed into her mind. The way Dr. Reynolds had spoken as if Iris were a case study, not a woman in a hospital bed. The steady hum of the machines, out of step with the rhythm of Iris's breaths. Even the lavender scent drifting through the halls stung like a plug-in left on high.

And Iris's room. Too staged. The bed was made with military precision, artwork placed perfectly, a vase of roses on the table—perfect and untouched. It didn't seem like a place for recovery. It was more of a showroom.

The monitor above Iris's bed had faltered, its lines jagged and uncertain. Reynolds had noticed. Sofia had seen the brief tightening of his jaw before he leaned over and adjusted the settings, smoothing the display as if nothing had happened.

By the time Sofia reached the exit doors, her certainty had sharpened. Something was wrong. Not just with Iris, but with the hospital itself.

On her walk home, Sofia turned these thoughts over in her mind, trying to make sense of them. Edenvale had always been perfect. Unchanging. Nobody ever left, and no one new ever came. Everyone was always just there. People didn't get sick. They didn't suffer in any way. But Iris had crashed. Iris was hurt. And now, for the first time, Sofia wondered if that perfection had been real at all, or if it was just a layer of the town's carefully painted illusion.

She stopped at the edge of the park, staring at the perfectly symmetrical flowerbeds and the neatly trimmed hedges. The colors were vibrant, almost unnaturally so, as if they'd been pulled from a painting. A breeze stirred the leaves, carrying with it a faint, artificial sweetness that made her stomach churn. This was an unfamiliar feeling for her.

For the first time in her life, Sofia felt... different. Out of sync with the world around her. The feeling was barely there, almost too slight to notice, but she felt it all the same. A quiet, gnawing sense that she no longer fit.

Back at her house, Sofia sat by the window, watching the townspeople go about their day. They were so predictable, so perfectly composed. She thought about the whispers she'd overheard earlier, the way they'd spoken about Iris as if she were an object of curiosity, not a person.

Sofia wondered what they'd say if they could read her thoughts. If they knew she was starting to question Edenvale's perfection.

The idea made her shiver.

In The Shadow of Perfection

The clock ticked softly in the background, its rhythm steady and unchanging. Yet as Sofia stared at it, she felt a strange disconnect. Time felt... off. The seconds seemed to stretch and blur. The ticking was almost too loud in the quiet of her home. She glanced at her reflection in the glass, and for a moment, she thought she saw someone else, a shadow or a flicker.

She spun, heart hammering, but the room was empty. The same spotless, orderly space it had always been. Sofia pressed a hand to her chest, dragging in a shaky breath. *You're just tired,* she told herself. *That's all.* But even as she said it, she knew it was a lie.

Chapter Twelve

As the days unfolded, Sofia found herself increasingly preoccupied with Iris. Not just the crash, but everything surrounding it—the art, the whispers, the gnawing feeling that Edenvale was no longer as flawless as it appeared. Iris's haunting, dark paintings had been at the center of conversations around town, and though no one openly admitted it, she could tell they made people uneasy.

In the privacy of her home, Sofia sat by the window, her gaze unfocused. The streets outside were as orderly as ever, the flowerbeds in full bloom, the children playing with a robotic, rehearsed energy. And yet something was wrong. Sofia was becoming aware of the seams in Edenvale's perfection, the tiny cracks that had always been there but had gone unnoticed.

Sofia couldn't sleep. She lay rigid in bed, eyes fixed on the ceiling while her thoughts spun in relentless circles. The hospital had shaken her more than she cared to admit. It wasn't just Iris. It was everything. Especially Dr. Reynolds.

"She's fighting something we can't see." The words replayed, over and over, slicing through her sense of order. Each echo chipped at the certainty she'd built her life on.

At last, the stillness became unbearable. She pushed back the covers and paced the living room, her bare feet whispering against the floor. Moonlight spilled through the window, laying pale patterns across the rug.

She stopped. Her gaze caught on the glass. Her own reflection stared back at her.

Was it her imagination, or did she look... different? Her skin seemed paler, her eyes hollowed by shadows she hadn't noticed before.

She leaned closer, fingertips brushing her cheek. Everything looked normal. Too normal. And still, the unease wouldn't leave her.

"You're overthinking," she whispered, the sound barely breaking the silence. "You just need sleep."

But even as the words left her lips, she knew they weren't true.

In The Shadow of Perfection

By the time morning arrived, Sofia had made up her mind. She would visit Iris's house. There was something there. Maybe there was something in those paintings that held the answers she was looking for. If Iris's art had changed so drastically, perhaps it was trying to tell a story, one that Iris herself couldn't share.

Sofia dressed quickly, her movements brisk but deliberate. She didn't bother with breakfast, her appetite long since replaced by a gnawing curiosity. As she grabbed her coat and stepped outside, the cool morning air prickled her skin. The streets were quiet, the town still wrapped in the haze of early dawn.

Iris's house stood at the edge of the square, modest and unassuming, almost lost behind the blaze of flowers and clipped hedges. On another day, the sight might have soothed Sofia. But under the heavy gray sky, the house gave off something else—an unsettling energy.

Sofia's steps slowed as she approached the front door. She hesitated, glancing over her shoulder, her heart hammering in her chest. She couldn't shake the feeling that someone was watching her. For a moment, her gaze lingered on the street. It was empty. The only thing she could hear was the faint hum of distant lawn sprinklers. No one was there, yet the sensation of unseen eyes prickled at the back of her neck. With a sharp breath, she crouched, reached beneath the mat, and pulled out the spare key Iris always kept there.

The key turned in the lock with a soft click, and the door creaked open. Sofia stepped inside, immediately engulfed by the scent of turpentine and paint. The house was quiet. Too quiet. The fridge didn't hum. The clock didn't tick. Not the tranquil quiet she'd expected, but a heavy, oppressive stillness that settled on her like a weight. The air seemed thicker inside.

The living room was immaculate, every cushion perfectly fluffed, every piece of furniture positioned with precision. It was so orderly it felt wrong, especially now, knowing Iris's world had been spiraling into chaos. Sofia's eyes darted to the mantel above the fireplace, where framed photos of the girls' nights and Iris's early gallery openings stood proudly. They stared back at her like relics from another lifetime. She swallowed hard. This wasn't why she was here.

The studio door at the end of the hallway was slightly ajar. Sofia's breath caught as she approached, her footsteps soft on the polished wood floors. She pushed the door open, and the scene inside made her freeze.

Chapter Thirteen

The studio was a stark contrast to the rest of the house. Chaos reigned here. Half-finished canvases leaned haphazardly against the walls. Some were smeared with dark, violent streaks of paint that bled over the edges. Paintbrushes lay scattered across the worktable, their bristles stiff and caked with dried pigment. Open jars of paint were scattered across the room. The once-bright white walls bore smudges and streaks of color, as though Iris had lashed out in a fit of frustration.

Sofia stepped cautiously into the room, her eyes scanning the mess. Her gaze was immediately drawn to the largest canvas propped on the easel. It depicted Edenvale, but not the Edenvale she knew. The town square was twisted, the buildings leaning at impossible angles. The fountain, usually the centerpiece of cheerful gatherings, was cracked and dry, its base littered with jagged stones. The sky was a stormy gray, heavy with swirling clouds that seemed alive. Shadowy figures lurked in the corners, half-formed and indistinct, as though they were trying to emerge from the darkness but couldn't quite break free.

Sofia's breath hitched. The painting wasn't just dark; it was oppressive. It felt alive, as though it were drawing her into its twisted world. She stepped closer, her fingers trembling as she reached out to touch the edge of the frame. The texture of the paint was rough, the strokes frenzied and chaotic. She whispered, almost to herself, "What were you trying to tell us, Iris?"

She turned her attention to a stack of papers on the cluttered worktable. The top sheet was a hurried sketch of the hospital, its sleek exterior marred by cracks that spider-webbed across its surface. The next sheet showed the town square again, this time completely abandoned. The buildings were intact, but their windows were hollow, and the fountain's water had turned black. Each subsequent sketch was darker, more abstract. Spirals and jagged lines consumed entire pages, interspersed with faces that seemed to dissolve into the paper itself.

Sofia scanned the room. The other canvases bore similarly haunting images. One showed a barren landscape—not Edenvale, but a different place. The ground was cracked, the trees skeletal. Another depicted a group of people standing in a circle, their faces obscured by dark smudges. Above them, faint shapes floated, like figures observing from a distance.

Sofia's stomach churned. She hadn't expected this. She'd thought Iris's art would provide answers, but instead, it only deepened the mystery. Her thoughts raced. Could the paintings be a warning? A vision? Or were they simply the product of a mind unraveling?

A glint of light caught her eye. She turned sharply, her breath hitching. Shiny stood propped against the far wall, its surface pristine despite the disarray around it. The mirror's smooth glass reflected the chaos of the studio, but as Sofia stepped closer, she froze. Her reflection stared back at her, but something was wrong. Behind her, in the depths of the mirror, shadows shifted.

"Sofia," Shiny said, its voice soft yet firm, breaking the heavy silence. She stepped back, her pulse racing.

"What do you want?" she whispered, her voice trembling.

"Search for the truth," Shiny replied. Its tone was calm, almost gentle, but there was an edge to it. "But tell no one. Not yet."

Sofia's hands clenched into fists. "Why?"

In The Shadow of Perfection

The mirror's surface rippled faintly, as though responding to her agitation. "They are watching," it said simply. "But not all of us are the same. Some of us see as Iris did."

Sofia's heart thudded painfully in her chest. "You mean... you're different?"

Shiny didn't answer directly. Instead, it whispered, "Find the other paintings."

"What paintings?" Sofia demanded, but Shiny had fallen silent. Her reflection stared back at her, the shadows behind her now still.

Sofia turned back to the room, her mind racing. She searched frantically, her hands shaking as she moved canvases and papers aside. At the very back of the stack, hidden beneath a cloth, she found them. The first canvas made her gasp.

It was a painting of a sterile room, its walls lined with screens. Figures in white lab coats stood in a semi-circle, their faces obscured by masks. On the screens were images of Edenvale—the town square, the hospital, the rows of perfect houses. The perspective was strange, as though the town were being observed from above.

In The Shadow of Perfection

Sofia's knees felt weak. She pulled the canvas closer, her fingers tracing the shapes on the screen. "What is this?" she whispered, her voice cracking.

The next painting showed Edenvale, but the buildings were translucent, their interiors visible. Inside each house, shadowy figures moved, their forms blurred as if they were being monitored. In the background, a faint outline of a dome encased the town, barely visible but undeniably there.

Sofia stepped back, her mind spinning. These weren't just paintings. They were... something else. Something Iris had seen, or imagined, or...

"They will come for you if they know you've seen this." Shiny's voice interrupted her thoughts, its tone sharper now. "Leave no trace."

Sofia's eyes darted to the door, her breath quickening. She grabbed her phone and snapped pictures of the paintings, her hands trembling so badly the images blurred. She didn't care. She had to leave. She had to get out before someone... before something found her here.

As she turned to go, her eyes fell on one last painting, smaller than the others. It was a portrait of Iris, but not the Iris she knew. This Iris looked older, worn, her face lined with worry. Behind her, the shadows loomed larger, almost engulfing her. In the reflection of her eyes, Sofia thought she saw... screens.

"Iris, what is all this you are trying to say? What does it mean? Who is watching us and why?" she demanded, her fear now mingled with a strange determination.

"Your questions are the right ones," Shiny said cryptically. "But the truth is dangerous. Take what you've found and tell no one."

Sofia stared at the mirror, her mind a swirl of confusion and unease. She glanced back at the canvases, then at Shiny, whose reflection now seemed unnervingly still. Without another word, she grabbed a large box from under the worktable and began carefully placing the canvases and sketches inside. Whatever this was, it wasn't safe here.

She carried the box to her car, her movements quick and deliberate. After securing it in the trunk, she reached into the back seat and pulled out a neatly packed basket of baked goods. It had been her cover, her reason for being here in case she saw someone and had to explain herself. She placed the basket on Iris's kitchen table, arranging it carefully before pausing to glance around the room.

In The Shadow of Perfection

As she turned to leave, there was a sharp knock at the door. Sofia froze, her heart racing.

The door creaked open, and Dr. Reynolds stepped inside, his expression one of mild surprise that quickly turned to suspicion. "Sofia," he said, his tone measured. "What are you doing here?"

She forced a smile, her hands clasping tightly in front of her. "I came to water Iris's plants and bring some baked goods for when she comes back. I thought it might cheer her up."

Dr. Reynolds's gaze swept the room, lingering for a moment on the studio door before returning to Sofia. "Thoughtful of you," he said, his voice carefully neutral. "Though I wasn't aware you had a key to her house."

Sofia's smile didn't waver. "Iris gave it to me ages ago, in case she ever needed someone to look after her garden. Why are you here, Doctor?"

He stepped farther inside, closing the door behind him. "We're preparing to discharge Iris tomorrow," he said smoothly. "I came to make sure her house was in order for her return."

Sofia's stomach tightened. The explanation seemed plausible, but something in his tone felt off—too rehearsed, too careful. His eyes flicked briefly toward the studio again, and Sofia's unease deepened.

"Well," she said brightly, taking a step toward the door, "I've done my part. I should let you finish up."

Dr. Reynolds didn't move, his expression unreadable. "You're a good friend to Iris, Sofia. I'm sure she'll appreciate your thoughtfulness."

Sofia nodded, her heart pounding as she slipped past him and out the door. Once outside, she forced herself to walk calmly to her car, but as soon as she was inside, she gripped the steering wheel tightly, her breaths shallow.

Through the rearview mirror, she saw Dr. Reynolds watching her from the window, his figure—a shadow against the light. For a heartbeat, she could have sworn his reflection in the glass smiled. A chill ran down her spine. She didn't know what he was hiding, but she was certain of one thing.

Whatever was happening in Edenvale, it was far more sinister than she'd imagined.

Chapter Fourteen

Sofia reached her house, her hands trembling as she fumbled with the key in the lock. Her breath came in short, sharp gasps, the lingering unease from Iris's house and the hospital clinging to her like a second skin. The street was quiet—the warm glow of streetlights spilling over perfectly trimmed lawns and hedges. But even in the stillness, she felt watched. There was a prickling sensation at the back of her neck that refused to fade.

The door swung open. She slipped inside and turned the lock with a decisive click. Curtains drawn tight, her movements hurried. The cheerful floral fabric mocked her unease, its brightness jarring against the cloud of dread pressing closer.

Inside, the silence deepened. The air felt heavy, charged, amplifying the pounding of her heart.

Her gaze slid to the mantel. Shiny stood there, its glass catching the faint glow of the lamp and scattering slivers of light across the walls. The sight made her stomach turn.

Sofia crossed the room and gripped its ornate frame. With a sharp twist, she turned it to face the wall. "I don't trust you," she muttered, her voice low and unsteady.

The words felt weak, hollow, and for a fleeting moment, she thought she heard a faint hum—a vibration from the mirror. She shook her head, pushing the thought aside. There was no time to dwell on paranoia. She had work to do.

She hurried back outside to retrieve the box from her car. The night air was cool against her flushed skin, but it did little to soothe her frayed nerves. With every step, she glanced over her shoulder, half-expecting someone to emerge from the shadows. The box felt heavier than before as she carried it inside, the weight of its contents pressing against her chest like a leaden secret.

Once inside, she locked the door again, twisting the deadbolt twice to be certain. She carried the box upstairs to her bedroom and into the walk-in closet, her sanctuary from prying eyes. The space was cramped but familiar, its shelves lined with neatly folded clothes and a row of polished shoes. She placed the box on the floor and sat cross-legged before it, the dim overhead light casting long shadows across the walls.

In The Shadow of Perfection

Sofia carefully removed the lid, her hands trembling. The first canvas she pulled out was larger than she had remembered. It depicted Edenvale's town square, but the cheerful familiarity of the scene was gone. The fountain in the center was cracked, its once-gushing waters replaced by a stagnant pool. The buildings leaned unnaturally, their windows dark and empty, as though the life within had been extinguished.

She traced the jagged lines of the painting with her fingertips, her heart sinking. This wasn't the Edenvale she knew. This was something else entirely—a distorted reflection, an unraveling of the perfection they all took for granted.

Digging deeper into the box, she uncovered more paintings. Each one was darker, more unsettling than the last. There were twisted, gnarled trees clawing at an overcast sky; faceless figures standing motionless in the shadows of crumbling buildings; and what looked like the hospital, its pristine facade fractured, with shadowy figures peering from the cracks. The details sent shivers down her spine. She couldn't imagine what state of mind Iris had been in to create such haunting images.

As Sofia worked through the box, a slim leather-bound journal slipped from between two sketchbooks and landed on her lap. She paused, her brow furrowing. She hadn't noticed it before. Her hands hesitated over its worn cover, the edges frayed as if it had been handled too many times in haste.

Taking a deep breath, she opened it. The first few pages were filled with hurried sketches of circuits and wires, annotated with cryptic phrases: *network*, *surveillance*, *control*. The jagged lines and fragmented words mirrored the chaos in Iris's paintings. The further she read, the more disjointed the notes became. Some pages were missing, torn out violently, leaving ragged edges behind.

One passage stood out. The handwriting was deliberate, almost forced, as if Iris had been struggling to form coherent thoughts:

The hospital isn't just a hospital. The doctor knows. He's hiding something. And Shiny... Shiny is part of it all.

Sofia's breath hitched. Her mind raced back to her visit to the hospital. Dr. Reynolds—his calm demeanor, his insistence that Iris needed rest, his careful deflection of her questions. It all felt too controlled, too calculated. The memory of Dr. Reynolds's smile surfaced unbidden, polished and practiced—the kind of smile meant to hide rot.

In The Shadow of Perfection

As she closed the journal, her resolve hardened. She needed to talk to Iris. Whatever was happening in Edenvale, Iris held the key. But how could she reach her? The town was small, its people watchful. And if Iris's suspicions about Shiny were true, then every move they made was being monitored.

Sofia's gaze drifted to the note she had scribbled earlier. She unfolded it, the hastily written words staring back at her:

Iris, we need to talk, but not here. When you're ready, meet me by the old pine trail. Bring nothing but yourself. Sofia.

She folded the note carefully and slipped it into her pocket. She had to find a way to deliver it without drawing attention. But even as she formulated her plan, a chill ran down her spine. If Shiny was truly as pervasive as Iris's notes suggested, then it wasn't just Iris who was being watched. Everyone in Edenvale was under surveillance. Including her.

The thought sent her heart racing. She turned to the box of paintings, her eyes scanning their dark, ominous images. What was Edenvale? Who was behind it? And why did it feel as though the answers were just out of reach, veiled by the very perfection that had once comforted her?

In The Shadow of Perfection

As she sifted through the sketches, her fingers brushed against another canvas. It was smaller than the others but even more unsettling. The scene depicted was unfamiliar at first: a stark, sterile room filled with monitors and scientists peering at screens. On the screens were views of Edenvale—the town square, the hospital, even the street where Sofia lived. Her stomach turned as the realization struck her. This wasn't just art. This was a window into something far more sinister.

Her thoughts spiraled. Iris had been right. The town was a lie, and they were all part of something they couldn't yet comprehend. But why? And for whom?

Sofia's resolve hardened further. She would deliver the note to Iris and get the answers they both needed. But as she stared at the haunting images before her, a new fear took root. What if it was already too late?

Outside, the wind howled softly, rustling the branches of the trees. The house was quiet, but the silence felt heavy, oppressive. Sofia thought about her living room, where Shiny stood facing the wall. The urge to check it, to see if it was still turned away, gnawed at her. But she didn't move.

Instead, she sat in the closet, the journal clutched tightly in her hands, and whispered to herself, "We'll find the truth, Iris. Whatever it takes."

In The Shadow of Perfection

The weight of the journal and the paintings was almost too much to bear, but Sofia knew there was no turning back. The note in her pocket felt like a lifeline—a fragile thread connecting her to the answers she so desperately sought. She just hoped that thread wouldn't snap before they could uncover the truth.

Chapter Fifteen

Sofia's day began with the type of energy she hadn't felt in a long time, though it was fueled more by anxiety than excitement. She had arrived at Iris's house hours before anyone else, her car loaded with baskets of baked goods, pitchers of freshly made lemonade, and bouquets of flowers she had picked from her garden. The house, quiet and immaculate, seemed to exhale in her presence, its stillness unnerving.

The kitchen became her sanctuary as she prepared for the small gathering. She laid out trays of buttery scones, flaky pastries, and delicate finger sandwiches. Each item was arranged with precision, as though the act of creating order in this chaotic situation could calm her racing thoughts. The table was covered with a crisp white cloth. The centerpiece—a vase of sunflowers that seemed almost too bright for the occasion.

Sofia couldn't stop her mind from wandering. The last time she had been in this kitchen, she had uncovered truths that left her unsettled. Now, Iris was coming home, and Sofia didn't know what to expect. The faint scent of turpentine lingered in the air, a ghost of Iris's artistic world, but the atmosphere felt heavier than ever.

The town's cobblestone streets, usually serene and untouched by chaos, were abuzz with quiet anticipation. Word of Iris's discharge had spread quickly, and a small crowd had already gathered outside her house by mid-afternoon. Some faces were etched with genuine concern, while others bore the thinly veiled curiosity of those hungry for gossip.

The first knock came just as Sofia was putting the finishing touches on the table. Rebecca, always punctual, entered with a warm smile and a covered dish. "Thought I'd add to the feast," she said, placing her casserole on the counter.

Sofia returned the smile, though it felt strained. "Thank you, Rebecca. It's good to see you."

Rebecca looked around the kitchen, her brows knitting together. "Everything looks wonderful, as always. But... How are you holding up? I can't imagine how strange this must be for you, being so close to Iris."

Sofia hesitated, choosing her words carefully. "It's been... a lot to process. I just want her to feel at home when she gets here."

In The Shadow of Perfection

Rebecca nodded, her concern genuine. "We all do. She's been through so much."

The next wave of visitors arrived shortly after. Mrs. Haverly, Mr. Bernard, and Diana filtered in, their chatter filling the space as they placed their contributions on the table. The conversations were polite but tinged with curiosity.

"Have you spoken to her since the accident?" Diana asked, her voice low as she leaned toward Sofia.

"Not much," Sofia admitted. "She's been recovering, and I didn't want to overwhelm her."

Mrs. Haverly shook her head. "Iris is strong. She'll bounce back. But I do wonder what she remembers. Accidents like that... they leave scars."

Sofia bit her lip, unsure how to respond. She stood at the edge of the living room, her hands twisting nervously as she listened to the hum of conversation around her. The house was alive with polite chatter, yet every word seemed to carry an undercurrent of curiosity veiled by concern. Plates of pastries and glasses of iced tea were clutched by neighbors who had come under the guise of welcoming Iris home but were clearly there to witness something extraordinary—or unsettling.

In The Shadow of Perfection

"Do you think she'll look... the same?" Mrs. Haverly asked in a hushed tone to Mr. Bernard, standing just a few feet from Sofia. Her lavender cardigan practically radiated innocence, but her voice carried a sharp edge of intrigue.

"I heard the hospital worked wonders," Mr. Bernard replied, his voice low but animated. "Dr. Reynolds is known for his... precision."

Diana, balancing a plate of lemon bars, joined in with a conspiratorial whisper. "Still, a crash like that? She must've been in pieces. It's almost unbelievable she's coming home so soon."

Sofia glanced at them out of the corner of her eye, her stomach twisting. She busied herself with straightening the refreshments on the table, trying to block out their voices, but they seemed to grow louder with every word.

"It's almost too good to be true," Rebecca murmured, her brow furrowed. "Do you think she remembers any of it? Or... maybe she's choosing not to."

Sofia's fingers tightened around the edge of the tablecloth. She didn't trust herself to join the conversation. The unease she had felt since Iris's accident had only deepened. Something about the entire situation felt orchestrated, like a play where everyone was sticking to a script they didn't even realize they were following. And the star of the show, Iris, was about to make her grand entrance.

Outside, the sound of a car pulling up drew the room to a hush. Conversations stopped mid-sentence as all heads turned toward the window. The sleek black vehicle gleamed under the afternoon sun, a striking contrast against the vibrant flowers of Iris's garden.

Sofia's breath hitched as the car door opened, and Dr. Reynolds stepped out first, his posture as impeccable as ever. He moved with the deliberate precision of someone accustomed to commanding attention. Then, with almost theatrical timing, Iris emerged. A hush rolled through the room before anyone remembered to breathe.

Iris looked radiant and flawless. Her skin was luminous, free of the faintest blemish or shadow. Her hair, once slightly unruly in its artistic charm, now fell in perfect waves over her shoulders. She wore a simple yet elegant dress that seemed to amplify the glow that surrounded her. Even her movements, as she stepped onto the path leading to the house, were fluid and deliberate, as if choreographed.

"She looks incredible," Diana breathed, her tone teetering between awe and disbelief.

In The Shadow of Perfection

"Better than ever," Rebecca agreed, her voice tinged with something Sofia couldn't quite place—envy, perhaps, or fear.

But Sofia didn't feel awe. She felt cold. This wasn't the Iris she knew. This wasn't the friend who had painted vivid, messy masterpieces or laughed uncontrollably at their inside jokes. This Iris was a polished version, a doll-like figure stepping into a role that didn't suit her.

The crowd erupted into polite applause as Iris approached the house, her smile wide and radiant. She waved gracefully, thanking everyone with a soft voice that carried just enough warmth to seem genuine. But Sofia caught something in her eyes—a flicker of detachment, as if Iris were watching herself from a distance.

"Welcome home, Iris!" Mrs. Haverly exclaimed, stepping forward to clasp Iris's hands. "You look absolutely stunning."

"Thank you, Mrs. Haverly," Iris replied, her voice smooth and melodic. "I feel wonderful."

"You're glowing," Diana added, her smile almost too eager. "It's like the accident never happened."

In The Shadow of Perfection

"Everything feels just as it should," Iris said, her gaze sweeping the crowd. "I'm so grateful to be back among all of you."

Sofia forced a smile as she stepped forward, carrying a tray of tea. "Here, Iris. You must be thirsty after the drive."

Iris turned to her, her smile never faltering. "Sofia. Always so thoughtful. Thank you."

Their eyes met, and for a fleeting moment, Sofia thought she saw something behind Iris's perfect facade—a glimmer of uncertainty, a crack in the mask. But it was gone as quickly as it appeared, replaced by that impossibly serene expression.

The afternoon unfolded like a scene from a play. Neighbors mingled, their compliments flowing freely as Iris navigated the room with practiced ease. Dr. Reynolds lingered near the edges, his sharp eyes missing nothing. Sofia watched him carefully, noting how he seemed to guide Iris subtly, steering her conversations and deflecting questions that veered too close to the accident.

"Dr. Reynolds," Sofia said, catching him as he poured himself a glass of lemonade. "You must be relieved to see Iris doing so well."

In The Shadow of Perfection

"Relieved, yes," he replied smoothly. "Though I must admit, her recovery has been remarkable. It's a testament to the care we provide in Edenvale."

Sofia held his gaze, searching for something in his expression. "And her memory? Has she been able to recall anything about the accident?"

Dr. Reynolds's smile didn't falter, but his eyes hardened just slightly. "Memory loss is common in cases of trauma. It's a protective mechanism, you understand. Best not to press her on it."

"Of course," Sofia said, though her unease deepened. She excused herself, retreating to the kitchen under the pretense of fetching more napkins. There, she gripped the edge of the counter, her mind racing.

This wasn't right. None of it was right. Iris's appearance, her demeanor, Dr. Reynolds's careful control. It all felt too perfect, too calculated. Sofia didn't believe in coincidences, and this was no exception.

As the crowd began to thin, Sofia felt a wave of relief. She stayed close to Iris, subtly guiding her away from lingering neighbors and their prying questions. As the last guest disappeared down the cobblestone path, Sofia let out a soft sigh of relief. The house, bustling with polite chatter and laughter just moments before, now felt unnervingly silent. She glanced at Iris, who stood by the kitchen counter, her flawless appearance so striking it was almost unsettling. The radiant glow of her skin, the gleam in her eyes—it all seemed too perfect, too polished, like a finely tuned instrument with no room for discord.

"Well," Iris said with a soft laugh, smoothing the skirt of her dress, "that was... overwhelming. But lovely, of course."

Sofia smiled, though her unease lingered. "Everyone was thrilled to see you. They've all been so worried."

Iris tilted her head, her expression serene. "Worried? About what? Everything is fine now, Dr. Reynolds said I'm perfectly recovered."

"Right," Sofia murmured, hesitating as she gathered the empty glasses from the coffee table. She had been trying to piece together Iris's behavior all afternoon, but nothing added up. This wasn't the Iris she knew—the artist with sharp wit and an ever-curious mind. This Iris was... polished, scripted even.

"Let me help," Iris said, reaching for a tray of leftover pastries. Her movements were graceful, almost mechanical, as though rehearsed. "You've done so much already, Sofia. Thank you for everything."

In The Shadow of Perfection

"Of course," Sofia replied, trying to keep her tone light. She wanted to ask so many questions, but the fear of pushing too hard kept her in check. Instead, she watched as Iris moved through her home, her smile unwavering, her demeanor unnervingly calm.

Sofia placed the empty glasses in the sink and dried her hands on a dish towel. "Iris, about the hospital..." she began cautiously. "Do you remember much from your stay there?"

Iris turned to her, her expression unchanging. "Not really. It was all a bit of a blur. But Dr. Reynolds was wonderful. He's so kind, isn't he?"

Sofia forced a smile. "Yes, he's... very attentive. But do you remember anything specific? Any conversations or... oddities?"

Iris's brow furrowed slightly, but the serene mask didn't slip. "Oddities? No, nothing like that. He made sure I was comfortable and pain-free. Honestly, it was almost like floating. No pain, no worries. Just... peace."

Sofia's stomach churned. Floating. Peace. The words felt wrong, too manufactured. She tried again, her tone as casual as she could manage. "And the accident? Do you remember anything about that night?"

In The Shadow of Perfection

Iris's gaze grew distant, as though searching for something just out of reach. Then she smiled, that same polished, detached smile. "Not much. Just flashes. But it doesn't matter, does it? What's important is that I'm fine now."

Sofia's heart sank. Iris's answers were too perfect, too rehearsed. It was as if someone had wiped away the edges of her personality, leaving only a smooth, sanitized version of the friend she once knew.

"I'm glad you're feeling better," Sofia said softly, though her mind raced with doubts. She hesitated, then ventured cautiously, "Would you mind if I stayed over tonight? Just to make sure you're settled? It's your first night back, after all."

Iris blinked, a flicker of something unreadable crossing her face before she shook her head gently. "That's so thoughtful of you, Sofia, but really, I'll be fine. Everything's back to normal now."

Back to normal. The phrase rang hollow in Sofia's ears. She nodded, masking her disappointment. "If you're sure."

"I am," Iris said firmly, her smile unwavering. "But thank you. It means so much to me that you've done all this. You're such a good friend."

In The Shadow of Perfection

Sofia's fingers tightened around the edge of the dish towel. She knew Iris wasn't dismissing her out of malice, but the rejection stung nonetheless. "Well, before I go, there's something I wanted to give you," she said, reaching into her pocket. She pulled out the folded note and handed it to Iris.

"What's this?" Iris asked, unfolding the paper.

"Just a little... idea I had," Sofia said carefully. "Read it when you have a moment. It's nothing urgent."

Iris's eyes scanned the note. For a brief moment, her serene expression faltered. She looked up at Sofia, a glimmer of something. Hesitation? Curiosity? Then, as quickly as it appeared, it was gone. She folded the note neatly and slipped it into her pocket.

"Thank you," she said, her tone as smooth as ever. "I'll take a look later."

Sofia nodded, forcing a smile. "Good. I'll... I'll leave you to rest, then."

As she gathered her things and prepared to leave, Sofia's mind raced. The note was a gamble, a desperate attempt to reach the real Iris buried beneath this perfect facade. She just hoped it would be enough.

In The Shadow of Perfection

When she stepped out into the cool night air, the weight of the day pressed heavily on her shoulders. The streets of Edenvale were quiet, the perfect stillness unsettling. She glanced back at Iris's house, its windows glowing warmly in the darkness. But the warmth felt like a lie, a veneer hiding something far colder.

Sofia's resolve hardened. Whatever was happening in Edenvale, she would uncover it. She had to.

Inside the house, Iris sat alone in the dimly lit living room. She unfolded the note once more, her fingers brushing over the words. A faint smile played on her lips, but her eyes remained distant, unreadable.

Outside, the wind whispered through the trees, carrying with it secrets yet to be revealed.

Chapter Sixteen

The days following Iris's return to Edenvale fell back into a rhythm so perfect, it bordered on the unnerving. The house, though still shadowed by the memories of her accident, was bright and pristine, as if the incident had never happened. Every vase was filled with fresh flowers delivered by well-meaning neighbors; the fridge was stocked with casseroles, soups, and carefully labeled containers of comfort food. Even the garden seemed to bloom with renewed vigor, as if nature itself had decided to contribute to her recovery.

Iris moved through her home with an ease that surprised even her. Her steps were light, her head clear, and the world outside her window seemed as serene as ever. Any aches or reminders of the crash had dissipated, and she found herself marveling at her apparent resilience. At times, she even forgot that she had been in an accident. Life in Edenvale was like that: seamless, polished, and untouched by hardship.

In The Shadow of Perfection

Yet at night, when the house settled into its stillness, the dreams began.

It started subtly, a flicker of warmth that enveloped her as soon as she closed her eyes. In her dream, Iris was seated in a cozy living room bathed in the golden glow of late-afternoon light. The furniture was inviting, a mix of soft cushions and worn wood that spoke of love and use. Children's laughter filled the air, pure and infectious, as a boy and a girl played on the carpet. They were building a tower of blocks, their tiny hands moving with focused determination, their voices chiming in playful arguments over which piece should go where.

Iris watched them from the couch, a contented smile spreading across her face. Her heart swelled with pride, a sensation so vivid it almost hurt. Beside her, a man sat with an easy confidence, his arm draped casually over her shoulders. His presence was warm and steady, his voice rich and familiar.

"They're incredible," he said, his tone laced with awe.

"They are," Iris replied, her voice soft with affection. "I just hope we're enough for them. That we're doing this right."

The man's grip on her shoulder tightened slightly, a reassuring squeeze. "We're more than enough," he said firmly. "They're happy, Iris. Look at them. They're happy because of you."

She turned her gaze back to the children. The boy's eyes shone with determination as he carefully placed the final block at the top of the tower, and the girl clapped her hands, her giggle lighting up the room. The sight filled Iris with a peace so profound that she never wanted to wake up.

But she did. Morning light filtered through the curtains, and Iris opened her eyes with a lingering sense of warmth. The dream lingered on the edge of her consciousness, vivid and bittersweet. She lay in bed for a moment, staring at the ceiling, replaying the scene in her mind.

Who were they? The man, the children? They felt so real, so familiar, yet she knew they couldn't be. She had no husband, no children. Her life was here, in Edenvale, among the neighbors who adored her and the art that had defined her. And yet a part of her ached, as though she had lost something precious.

Iris shook her head, chastising herself. How could she miss something she never had?

By mid-morning, she was back in her studio. The scent of turpentine and fresh canvas wrapped around her like an old friend. It had been weeks since she had picked up a brush, and the absence had left a void she hadn't fully realized until now. The room, once chaotic with half-finished works, had been carefully tidied in her absence. The blank canvases leaned against the walls like quiet invitations, waiting for her to give them life.

She hesitated at first, her hand hovering over the palette. What would she paint? Edenvale, of course. It was always Edenvale—its golden streets, its perfect gardens, its smiling faces. But when the brush touched the canvas, it wasn't Edenvale that emerged.

The strokes were soft at first, tentative, but they quickly grew bolder. She painted a room—not her studio, not any room she had ever seen in Edenvale. It was the living room from her dream, cozy and filled with light. The children appeared next, their tiny forms rendered in careful detail, their laughter almost audible as she brought them to life on the canvas. And then the man. His strong jaw, his kind eyes, the way his hand rested on her shoulder. Finally, she painted herself, nestled beside him, her expression one of contentment and love.

When she stepped back to look at the painting, a lump formed in her throat. It was beautiful. It was perfect. And it wasn't hers. Not in any way that mattered. She didn't know these people. They didn't exist. And yet staring at them, she felt as though they had been a part of her for a lifetime.

Iris sat on the stool, her hands resting in her lap, and let out a shaky breath. "Who are you?" she whispered, her voice trembling. The painted figures offered no answers, only silent smiles that seemed to hold secrets she couldn't begin to unravel.

The rest of the day passed in a haze. She moved through her routines, but her thoughts kept drifting back to the family on the canvas. She found herself smiling at the memory of their laughter, their warmth. And then just as quickly, the smile would fade, replaced by a gnawing sense of loss.

As evening fell, she stood in the kitchen, staring out the window at the perfectly manicured garden. Her reflection in the glass caught her off guard. For a moment, she thought she saw a flicker of movement behind her, a shadow that didn't belong. She turned quickly, her heart pounding, but the room was empty.

The air felt heavier now, charged with something she couldn't name. Iris took a deep breath, her fingers curling into fists. She couldn't let herself spiral. Not again. This was just a dream, just a painting. Nothing more.

In The Shadow of Perfection

As she climbed into bed that night, the warmth of the dream returned, wrapping around her like a blanket. She closed her eyes, and the family appeared again, their faces etched with love and joy. And somewhere deep inside, a voice whispered a truth she wasn't ready to face: "You knew them once. You loved them once."

Iris woke with a start, her chest heaving, her heart racing. The clock on her nightstand read 3:15 a.m. The house was silent, but her mind was loud, the echoes of the dream refusing to fade. She sat up, running a hand through her hair, and glanced at the studio door. The painting waited there, a reflection of a life she didn't remember.

She swung her legs over the side of the bed and stood, her bare feet cold against the wooden floor. The house felt different in the quiet hours of the night, as though it were holding its breath, waiting for her to make a move.

Iris walked to the studio, her steps slow and deliberate. She turned on the light, and there it was—the family, frozen in their moment of happiness, staring back at her with eyes that seemed to see too much.

She reached out, her fingers brushing the edge of the canvas. "Who are you?" she asked again, her voice barely more than a whisper. This time, she wasn't sure if she was speaking to the painting or herself.

Chapter Seventeen

Late-afternoon sunlight slipped through the blinds, striping the studio floor. Iris sat cross-legged, her phone propped on a paint-smeared stool. Ochre and blue clung to her fingers, stubborn traces of the work she couldn't leave alone.

On the canvas, a family had begun to form—a husband, a wife, two children standing in a park. Their faces were unfinished, blurred at the edges. Yet the closeness was clear in the small details: the tilt of a head, the near touch of hands.

Iris's chest tightened as she stared at them. The feeling was sharp, almost painful, a longing she couldn't explain. These people were not part of her life. They were not part of Edenvale. They didn't belong in her memories.

In The Shadow of Perfection

Still, they felt real, as if pulled up from a part of her she wasn't meant to access.

Iris gripped her phone, thumb hovering over Sofia's name. The house was silent, except for the faint hum of Shiny in the corner, its glass catching the low light.

A heaviness pressed against her chest. The dreams. The paintings. Faces she felt tied to but couldn't place. People she didn't know—yet somehow missed.

Before she could change her mind, she hit *Call*.

Sofia answered on the second ring, her voice warm but cautious. "Iris? Is everything okay?"

"I..." Iris hesitated, glancing over her shoulder at Shiny. She lowered her voice instinctively, though the house was empty. "I just needed to talk to someone."

Sofia's tone softened. "Of course. I'm here. What's going on?"

Iris took a shaky breath, unsure how to start. "It's these dreams I've been having... They're so vivid, Sofia. It's like I'm remembering something, but that doesn't make sense."

Sofia paused, the line crackling faintly in the silence. "What kind of dreams?"

In The Shadow of Perfection

"There's a family," Iris said slowly, choosing her words with care. "A man, two children—a boy and a girl. I could see them so clearly. I could hear their laughter. It felt... familiar. Like they were a part of me. But it can't be. I don't have a family like that."

Sofia didn't respond immediately. She moved to the window, pulling the curtain aside just enough to peer out into the quiet street. Her eyes flicked to her own Shiny, deliberately turned to face the wall, its presence still unnerving.

"That's strange," Sofia said finally, her voice carefully measured. "Maybe your mind is trying to tell you something. Dreams can be tricky like that."

"It's more than that," Iris pressed, her voice trembling. "I started painting them, Sofia. I couldn't stop myself. All of my new paintings... They're not images of Edenvale. They're of this family, this... life. It doesn't feel like a dream; it doesn't feel made up. It feels real."

Sofia's stomach knotted. She stepped farther from the window, lowering her voice. "Iris, have you told anyone else about this? Anyone at all?"

"No," Iris said quickly. "Who would I tell? It seems like everyone just wants things to go back to normal. They don't want to hear about strange dreams or paintings that don't make sense. Besides, I doubt anyone else would understand. That is why I called you; you have always been there for me."

Sofia nodded to herself, her suspicions deepening. "Good. Don't tell anyone. Not yet. Not until we figure out what this means."

"We?" Iris asked, her voice catching slightly.

"Yes. We!" Sofia said firmly. "You're not alone in this. But, Iris, you need to be careful. I think... I think someone's watching us," she whispered.

Iris drew a sharp breath. "Watching us? What do you mean?"

Sofia hesitated, choosing her words carefully. "I can't explain everything right now. But it's safer if we talk in person. Somewhere private. Do you remember where we went before your first gallery exhibit? That little hiking spot outside town?"

Iris frowned, trying to recall. "The trail near Pine Ridge?"

"Yes," Sofia said, her voice quick and urgent. "Meet me there tomorrow morning at seven. Just the two of us. No phones, no distractions. We'll talk properly then."

"Why not here?" Iris asked, her unease growing.

In The Shadow of Perfection

Sofia's laugh was short and brittle. "Let's just say I've developed a very practical mistrust of walls."

Iris hesitated, her hand brushing the edge of her latest painting, the image of the laughing children and the man beside them. "All right," she said finally. "Tomorrow morning."

"Good," Sofia said, relief evident in her voice. "Pack lightly. Just the essentials. And, Iris…"

"Yes?"

"Don't tell anyone," Sofia said firmly. "Not even in passing. Trust no one."

The words sent a shiver down Iris's spine. "I won't," she promised.

As they ended the call, Sofia stared at her phone for a long moment before setting it down on the counter. She pulled her sweater tighter around her, the unease settling deeper into her bones. Something about Iris's dreams felt like a key, a piece of a puzzle neither of them fully understood.

In her room, Iris set her phone aside, her fingers trailing over the image she had painted. Her heart ached with a yearning she didn't comprehend. The children's faces seemed to glow in the dim light, their eyes holding a warmth that felt like home.

"How can you miss something you've never had?" she whispered to herself.

Shiny, its reflective surface gleaming faintly, remained silent. But in her mind, Iris could almost hear its voice, steady and insistent: "You have to remember, Iris."

The words lingered, filling the quiet house with a tension she couldn't escape.

Chapter Eighteen

Iris began packing for the hike. Pulling a small duffel bag from her closet, she methodically gathered her supplies: a pair of sturdy boots, a light jacket, a water bottle, a flashlight, and a compact sleeping bag. Each item she placed in the bag felt like a step closer to something she couldn't define—an answer, perhaps, or an inevitable confrontation.

As she packed, her gaze wandered to her latest painting, resting on the easel in her studio. The family stared back at her: the man with his warm, steady eyes, the boy and girl with their bright laughter captured in frozen brushstrokes. Her own image sat among them, her painted smile serene and content. A pang of longing hit her chest, sharp and unexpected.

She ran her fingers along the edge of the canvas. *How can I miss something I never had?*

The thought stayed with her as evening closed in. She sat on the sofa, her body heavy, her mind restless.

In The Shadow of Perfection

Somewhere between one breath and the next, her eyes slipped shut into a late-afternoon nap. And the dream pulled her into a world that wasn't hers.

She dreamed.

Fluorescent lights hummed overhead, their glare bouncing off spotless white surfaces. The smell of antiseptic hung heavy in the air, sharp enough to turn her stomach. Iris sat at a desk stacked with files, each one neatly labeled. Her fingers moved with practiced ease, flipping through a thick document. The title at the top made her throat tighten—*Cognitive Reconstruction Trials: Subject IR-105.*

The name gripped her. It felt familiar, like a word spoken too often to a stranger who shouldn't be one. Her eyes scanned the dense lines of text, but the scientific terms blurred, the charts and graphs dissolving into incomprehensible patterns.

Behind her, a voice broke the sterile silence.

"Iris, you're pushing yourself too hard. You've been at this for weeks."

She turned, and her breath hitched. A man stood there, his features slightly blurred at the edges, as though her mind couldn't fully grasp his image. But his voice was clear—warm, steady, and laced with concern.

In The Shadow of Perfection

"Dr. Corwin," she said, her tone resolute.

"How many times do we have to go over this? You can call me Elias," he said in a calm, measured voice.

"Elias, you know I can't stop now. We can't stop now. We're so close. If the Eden Project works, we could redefine how trauma is treated. Entire lives could be rebuilt."

Elias Corwin stepped closer, his expression troubled. "But at what cost?"

Iris bristled, turning back to the documents in front of her. "It's worth it," she said firmly. "We're giving people a second chance. A life without pain, without grief. Isn't that enough?"

Elias sighed, his voice heavy with unspoken fears. "And what about the lives we're erasing in the process? The truths they'll never know?"

She stayed silent. Her hands moved on their own, shuffling through the charts, but the data blurred. Numbers, lines, graphs—nothing held meaning.

The machines seemed louder now, their hum swelling into a constant, relentless buzz. Her chest tightened. Her breath quickened.

In The Shadow of Perfection

The lab dissolved into darkness, edges blurring until nothing was left but shadow.

"Iris." The voice snapped her awake. "Iris." Steady. Insistent.

Her eyes fixed on Shiny. The mirror gleamed in the dim light, its surface too vivid, too alive.

"Iris. Stay with me," it said. The words slid through her, cold enough to raise goosebumps.

Her pulse quickened. "Who are you?" The whisper barely escaped her throat.

The glass rippled. Something shifted beneath the surface, unseen. "Iris." The voice again. Firm. Familiar.

Her breath caught. She knew that tone.

"Elias?" The name slipped out before she could stop it.

The mirror stilled. No answer. Just the gleam of glass, mocking her silence.

Fragments from the dream crowded back—the lab, the files, the voice. None of it made sense. Yet all of it felt real.

"Shiny," she tried again, her voice trembling. "What are you hiding? What do you know?"

In The Shadow of Perfection

The surface shivered faintly, then went still. No reply. Iris stared, heart pounding, as if waiting for her own reflection to betray her.

Her thoughts spun. Were the dreams memories? Had she known Elias Corwin before? And why did Shiny sound like him?

The weight of it pressed down, threatening to crush her. Yet beneath the fear, a spark caught hold. She couldn't dismiss it. Not as coincidence. Not as imagination. Something was buried in her mind, and she needed to drag it to the surface.

She swung her legs off the sofa, movements deliberate. She reached for the notebook on the coffee table. Her hand shook, but the pen moved steadily enough to capture as many details as she could. Every line was a lifeline to the truth.

Cognitive Reconstruction Trials.

The Eden Project.

Dr. Elias Corwin.

Trauma.

Lives rebuilt.

Lives erased.

In The Shadow of Perfection

Her pen hovered, the blank lines staring back like a dare. She drew a long breath, then shut the notebook with a snap.

Tomorrow, she would meet Sofia. They would head for the mountains, beyond Edenvale's eyes, beyond its perfection.

The clock ticked on, each beat winding her tighter. Fear. Hope. Both tangled in her chest.

Whatever waited out there, she would face it.

What she didn't know was that something was already waiting for her.

Chapter Nineteen

Iris knew sleep wouldn't come. It never did after an afternoon nap. Evening pressed in, but her mind wouldn't quiet. The dreams kept circling, fragments that refused to fit. She pushed herself to her feet, shaking her head. Sitting here wouldn't bring answers. Not tonight.

In the kitchen, Iris poured coffee into a thermos, the sharp aroma dragging her back into the present. But when she returned to the studio, the canvas pulled her under again.

The figures stared at her: the boy with the cheeky grin, the girl's bright eyes, the man's steady gaze. And there she was—smiling among them.

Her throat tightened. *Was she a mother? Someone's wife?*

"Who are you?" she whispered to the painting, her voice shaking. "Where are you?"

In The Shadow of Perfection

The silence pressed in, heavy and accusing.

Her eyes slid to Shiny. "What do you know?" she breathed.

The mirror gleamed back at her, blank and innocent, yet alive with something she couldn't name. The memory of Elias's voice crawled across her skin.

"You said you needed me." Her voice hardened. "Why? What am I supposed to do?"

Nothing. Only her own reflection stared back, fractured with doubt.

As Iris packed away the last items for the trip, a knock at the door startled her. She froze, her heart racing. Edenvale was a town of routine, and unexpected visits were rare, especially at nine o'clock. She cautiously peeked through the window before she opened the door.

Sofia stood on the porch, her expression a mix of concern and determination. She held a small bundle in her arms, extra gear for their hike, no doubt.

"Sofia, what's going on? Has something happened?" Iris asked, opening the door. "I thought we agreed to meet in the morning."

In The Shadow of Perfection

Sofia stepped inside, her eyes scanning the room as if searching for something or someone. "I couldn't wait," she admitted. "I wanted to make sure you were okay."

Iris gestured toward the kitchen. "Of course. I'm fine. I'm just getting everything ready. Would you like some coffee?"

Sofia shook her head. "No, thanks. I won't stay long. I just... I had to see you."

Her tone was uncharacteristically tense, and Iris studied her closely. "Is everything all right?"

Sofia hesitated, her gaze drifting to Shiny. "I've been thinking about our conversation. About your dreams. And... I'm worried."

Iris frowned. "Worried? Why?"

Sofia lowered her voice, glancing over her shoulder as if someone might overhear. "Iris, I think you're remembering something. Something important. But I also think it's dangerous."

A chill ran down Iris's spine. "Dangerous?"

Sofia nodded. "I don't know what's going on, but this trip has to happen. We need to get away from here, away from..." Her eyes flicked toward Shiny as she whispered. "All of this."

In The Shadow of Perfection

Sofia reached into her pocket and pulled out a small, folded piece of paper. She handed it to Iris, her fingers brushing against hers. "Take this," she said quietly. "It has the details and driving directions for tomorrow. Remember, not a word to anyone."

Iris took the note. "Sofia, you're making me nervous."

Sofia gave her a brief hug, then stepped back. "Get some rest. We'll figure this out together. I'll see you tomorrow."

As the door closed behind her, Iris unfolded the note, her hands trembling.

The phone rang, its shrill tone slicing through the quiet of the house. Iris hesitated for a moment before picking it up. The number on the screen made her stomach lurch.

Dr. Reynolds.

She steadied herself, pressing the phone to her ear. "Hello?"

"Iris," Dr. Reynolds's smooth voice came through the line, warm but precise. "I apologize for the late call. I just wanted to check in and see how you're settling back in."

In The Shadow of Perfection

Her grip on the phone tightened. "I'm fine. Everything is great, actually. Never been better."

"That's wonderful to hear," he said, his tone carrying an undercurrent of professional satisfaction. "We're all so pleased with your recovery. It's truly remarkable how well you're doing."

Iris forced a laugh, the sound hollow even to her own ears. "Well, I have all of you to thank for that. The care I received was... exceptional."

"Yes," he agreed, a pause hanging heavily before he continued. "And your return home? The transition hasn't been too overwhelming?"

"Not at all," she lied, her gaze drifting toward Shiny in the corner of the living room. Its surface caught the light, gleaming innocently, though she couldn't shake the feeling it was listening. "I've slipped right back into my routine. Everything feels... normal."

"That's excellent," Dr. Reynolds said, but his tone sharpened slightly, like a scalpel cutting through pleasantries. "Iris, if you ever need anything—someone to talk to or more time to rest, my door is always open."

"Thank you, Doctor," she replied quickly, eager to end the conversation. "But really, I'm fine. There's nothing to worry about."

In The Shadow of Perfection

"Of course," he said, though his voice carried a note of skepticism. "Still, it's good to check in. We wouldn't want you to overexert yourself."

"I appreciate your concern," Iris said, her fingers drumming anxiously on the countertop. "But I have everything under control."

"Good to hear. And again, I apologize for the late call. I just wanted to make sure you are recovering well." There was a pause, as if he were weighing his next words. "Take care of yourself, Iris. Truly."

"I will," she assured him, her tone clipped. "Thank you for calling."

She ended the call before he could say more, her chest tight as she set the phone down.

His voice clung to her, smooth and practiced, like he'd rehearsed every word. He appeared concerned, but was it too much? Too controlled?

Reynolds had always unsettled her. At her welcome-home gathering, he hadn't joined the chatter or the laughter. He'd stood back, watching, his eyes skimming the room like he was taking notes.

Now, with his words echoing in her head, Iris felt it again—that prickle at the back of her neck. Iris shook her head, pushing the unease aside. No point feeding it now. She had to focus on tomorrow's hike.

An hour later, she was still awake, staring at the ceiling. The note lay hidden in her bag, but its message wouldn't leave her alone. Why the secrecy? Why couldn't she trust anyone? What had Sofia meant? Who was watching her?

Sleep crept in slowly, her mind knotted with questions, anticipation, and a fear she couldn't name.

Chapter Twenty

Morning broke sharp and clear over Edenvale. Sofia's hands trembled slightly as she slipped the unmarked box into the trunk of her car, concealing it beneath an old blanket. She cast a quick glance over her shoulder toward the house, where the silhouettes of her husband and children moved behind the curtains. Her husband, Mark, was engrossed in his morning routine, utterly unaware of the secrets she was carrying.

Luck had been on her side these past few days. Mark's camping trip with the children had given her just enough time to prepare, to hide what she had discovered, and to make sure he wouldn't suspect anything.

"Just a girls' hike, nothing serious," she had told him. But this wasn't just a hike.

The air was crisp as Sofia drove through Edenvale's empty streets. Mist clung low, softening the edges of the neat houses until they looked unreal, like a painting smudged at the corners.

In The Shadow of Perfection

Ahead, Pine Ridge rose, its trees tall and watchful, like guards at a gate. Sofia pulled over at the trailhead. For a moment, she sat still, gripping the wheel, listening to the tick of the cooling engine.

Finally, she stepped out. The cold mountain air bit at her skin, but it did nothing to calm the unease running through her.

Minutes later, Iris's car pulled up. She looked brighter today, her posture more relaxed, but Sofia noticed the subtle tension in her eyes—the kind that lingered even in laughter.

"Ready?" Sofia asked, adjusting the straps of her backpack.

"As I'll ever be," Iris replied, managing a small smile.

They set off into the woods, gravel crunching under their boots. For a while, only their footsteps and the occasional bird call disturbed the air. The trail wound between tall pines, sunlight piercing through the canopy in narrow, watchful beams.

The woods seemed peaceful. Yet something in the air said otherwise.

The path narrowed as they went deeper. Leaves carpeted the ground, muffling their steps. The shade grew colder. Each snap of a twig sounded sharp, out of place.

For a while, they walked in silence, the kind that felt necessary. Finally, Iris spoke. "It's strange being out here. Away from everything."

Sofia gave a short laugh. "Feels like we're sneaking off, doesn't it? Like we shouldn't be here."

Iris nodded slowly. "Yeah. Like we're breaking some unspoken rule."

They continued for a while, the forest closing in around them. The deeper they went, the more Iris felt the weight of the town lifting—and something else settling in its place.

Iris broke the silence. "Okay, what is all the secrecy about? And why couldn't we talk about things when we were at my house?"

Sofia abruptly stopped, grabbing Iris's hand with a firmness that startled her. "You trust me, right?"

"With my life." Iris's voice was steady, but her pulse quickened.

Sofia leaned in, her voice dropping to a whisper. "Call me crazy, but I think someone is watching us... all the time."

In The Shadow of Perfection

"Someone? Who?" Iris's voice wavered.

"I don't know if it's someone or something. But I have this feeling—we're not just being watched. We're being listened to. That's why I didn't feel safe talking at your house."

Iris swallowed hard. "I kind of get the same feeling. But I brushed it off. I thought I was just paranoid after the accident."

Sofia's eyes searched Iris's face. "Do you remember anything else? About the accident? About the hospital?"

Iris hesitated. "Flashes. I remember the feeling of falling, and glass shattering. I know it sounds crazy, but I heard voices. They were muffled, saying things I didn't understand. Then nothing. Waking up in that hospital room. I remember Dr. Reynolds—he was smiling at me like nothing had happened."

Sofia's jaw tightened. "Did he ever explain why the crash happened, or what exactly happened?"

Iris shook her head. "No. He just kept saying not to worry and to get some rest. And what's strange is that no one even talks about it anymore. Like it never happened. Even I feel... disconnected from it. And the dreams. They feel more real than the accident."

In The Shadow of Perfection

Sofia slowed her pace. "What else happened in the hospital? Can you remember anything else?"

Iris looked ahead, eyes narrowing. "Every time I asked questions, Dr. Reynolds would press this button connected to my IV. Moments later, I'd feel overwhelmingly tired—like I was floating away. And when I woke up, I couldn't remember anything. But now, fragments are coming back, mostly in dreams."

Sofia's voice dropped to a near whisper. "Iris... these aren't just dreams."

Iris froze. "Oh my gosh, you sound just like Shiny."

Sofia shook her head. "No, I'm serious. These can't be dreams. You're remembering something. It is probably something they don't want you to remember."

Iris's breath quickened. "I've thought about that. But why would anyone want to erase my memories? What could possibly be that important? And who are they? Who is watching us?"

Sofia's gaze darkened. "That's what we need to figure out. Do you remember anything unusual about the hospital staff? Visitors?"

Iris frowned. "There was a nurse. She never spoke to me directly, but she was always there, watching. And there was a man in a dark suit... I thought he was from the hospital, but he never wore a badge."

Sofia's grip tightened on her backpack strap. "Iris, what if this isn't about your accident? What if it's about something you knew before? Something they're trying to bury?"

A chill ran down Iris's spine. "But I can't remember anything."

Sofia glanced around the trees as if expecting to see eyes staring back. "That's exactly why it's dangerous. You don't know what you've forgotten."

They continued walking in tense silence, the forest around them thickening. The trail narrowed, branches clawing at their sleeves.

"Iris," Sofia said slowly, "have you noticed anything strange about Edenvale? Changes in people? Do you feel like anyone is acting differently around you?"

Iris hesitated. "Everyone seems... too perfect. They all seem oblivious to any changes or anything suspicious, which is why it makes it so hard to ask anyone anything or even trust anyone. They are either acting as if they don't notice anything or are somehow blinded and don't see what you and I see."

Sofia nodded grimly. "Exactly. And the Shiny devices? They're everywhere. Watching, listening. I tried turning mine off once, but it wouldn't let me. Said it was for my safety."

Iris paled. "Mine has been acting strange. And lately, it feels like it's responding to thoughts I haven't spoken aloud."

Sofia stopped. "Your Shiny actually told me it was different from the rest of them."

"What? When?" asked Iris, surprised.

"Remember when I was stopping by your house to water your plants when you were in the hospital and I had a couple of interactions with your Shiny. It basically said that they are there to watch, listen, and report, but it also said that yours is different from the rest of them. It almost seemed like it was trying to convince me it was on our side. But I don't think we can trust it. We can't trust anyone in town," said Sofia.

"I am so relieved that you had the same feeling too. I can't imagine what it would have been like if I couldn't share all of this with anyone. Especially about these dreams," Iris said.

"But what if they really aren't dreams? What if you are remembering something, something Dr. Reynolds or whoever else doesn't want you to remember for some inexplicable reason?"

"Actually, I kind of have the same feeling; the dreams... they just feel so real," Iris said.

"And this town?" Sofia interrupted. "Doesn't it feel different to you? Like people are watching. Listening. Even at home, I feel it. Like I'm not alone, even when I am."

Iris slowed her pace, thinking. "Since I got back, everything feels... polished. Too perfect. Like Edenvale's a painting, and we're stuck inside it. But sometimes, I catch something out of place. A crack in the canvas."

Sofia gave her a sidelong glance. "What kind of crack?"

Iris's voice dropped. "Dr. Reynolds. The way he looks at me. Like he's waiting for something. And Shiny, last night, I swear it spoke to me in someone else's voice. A man's voice. It sounded like someone from my dreams."

Sofia stopped in her tracks. "What did it say?"

Iris met her eyes. "It told me to try and remember. It said what you just said, that these aren't just dreams."

"You said it sounded like a man's voice, not Shiny's usual tone?" asked Sofia.

In The Shadow of Perfection

"Yes, it was definitely a man's voice," Iris confirmed.

"Did you recognize the voice?" Sofia was getting more curious.

"Yes, I think it was Dr. Elias Corwin," she said.

"Who is that? Do you know anyone by that name?" Sofia asked.

"That's just the thing. He is a guy from another dream I had," said Iris.

"Wait. What dream? You told me just about the family dream," insisted Sofia.

"I couldn't really make sense of the other dream, that's why I didn't tell you, but I wrote down some details I remembered from it. Actually, I brought my notes, I thought maybe you could help me decipher it." Iris sounded hopeful, yet worried.

Sofia's face paled. For a long moment, neither of them spoke.

Sofia exhaled slowly. "We need to figure this out. But not here. Not yet."

They continued walking, deeper into the woods. Hours passed, the forest thickening around them. The sun hung low in the sky, casting long, golden shadows across the forest floor. Finally, the trail looped back, guiding them to a secluded clearing near where they had parked.

"This looks like a good spot to set up camp," Sofia said, forcing a steadiness into her voice.

Iris nodded, still lost in thought.

They worked quietly, putting up the tent, unrolling sleeping bags and stacking firewood. The forest around them darkened as the sun dipped below the horizon, the air cooling with the approaching night.

Sofia stole a glance at Iris, who sat staring into the trees, her face unreadable. A cold breeze whistled through the trees.

"Let's get this fire going before it gets too cold and dark," Iris said.

"Yes, and you will need some light to see what I brought for you," Sofia said.

Iris nodded, her mind still racing. They gathered sticks and kindling, working in silence until the fire crackled to life, casting flickering light on the trees around them. The forest seemed to press in closer, the air heavy with unspoken fears.

In The Shadow of Perfection

The silence between them felt heavier now, like the trees themselves were holding their breath.

Sofia stared into the flames, her face unreadable. She stood up suddenly. "I'm going to grab something from the car. I'll be right back."

Iris glanced up, confused. "What is it?"

Sofia hesitated, her eyes flicking toward the darkening trail. "Just... something I think you need to see. Stay here."

Sofia disappeared down the path, swallowed by the trees. Iris watched the shadows stretch longer, creeping across the ground. The forest seemed to quiet down, even the birds falling silent.

Minutes passed. Then there was a sound, soft but distinct. Footsteps. But not from Sofia's direction.

Iris's breath caught. She turned slowly toward the trees, heart pounding.

"Hello?" she called out, voice barely above a whisper.

No answer. Only the rustle of leaves.

Then, from the darkness, a figure shifted. Watching.

Chapter Twenty-One

Iris's pulse roared in her ears as the fire crackled weakly beside her.

Sofia's voice called from the trail, distant but near. "Iris?"

But Iris couldn't move. Her eyes were locked on the figure just beyond the trees—still, silent, waiting.

Then it was gone.

Sofia emerged from the shadows of the trail, the box clutched tightly to her chest, her breath slightly uneven from the effort. Her eyes immediately locked onto Iris, who was standing stiffly by the fire, her face pale and her gaze fixed on the edge of the forest.

"Iris?" Sofia asked, her voice soft but urgent.

Iris didn't respond. Her hand was raised, trembling, pointing toward the dense line of trees just beyond their camp.

In The Shadow of Perfection

Sofia set the box down carefully, her pulse quickening. "What is it? What happened?"

"There was… someone," Iris whispered, her voice barely audible. "Standing right there. Watching me."

Sofia's breath caught. She turned her head slowly to where Iris was pointing, but all she could see were the darkened woods. Shadows danced across the trunks, cast by the flickering firelight, but the forest remained still.

"Are you sure?" Sofia asked, forcing herself to keep her voice steady. "It could've been… an animal. Or maybe just the shadows playing tricks. My walk to the car and back seemed a lot longer in the dark."

Iris shook her head, her eyes never leaving the spot. "No. It wasn't an animal. It wasn't the trees. It was a person. I saw them, Sofia. They were just standing there. Watching."

Sofia glanced back toward the trail, then toward the box she had just retrieved. Her stomach churned as the thought crossed her mind. Had someone followed her? Had they been seen?

"Okay," Sofia said finally, her voice firmer than she felt. "Let's sit by the fire. We'll keep it burning bright.

In The Shadow of Perfection

Whatever or whoever it was, they're gone now. We're safe."

Iris hesitated, but eventually nodded. She sat down by the fire, her knees drawn to her chest, her eyes darting to the shadows that seemed to stretch endlessly beyond their small circle of light.

Sofia moved closer, adding more kindling to the fire until it blazed higher, casting warmth and illumination across the camp. She took a seat beside Iris, her hand brushing against the box. She wanted to say something comforting, to offer reassurance, but the unease she felt made her words stick in her throat.

The night seemed heavier now, the usual forest sounds muted as if the woods themselves were holding their breath. Every rustle of leaves, every snap of a distant twig sent both women's eyes darting toward the darkness. The fire popped and hissed, and in the silence that followed, Iris realized the crickets had stopped.

Sofia finally broke the silence, her voice low. "Whatever this is, we're not facing it alone. We'll figure it out together."

Iris nodded, but her eyes stayed distant, haunted by the figure she thought she'd seen.

In The Shadow of Perfection

Above, the sky had sunk into darkness. Stars flickered weakly through the thick canopy, their light smothered before it reached the ground. And somewhere beyond the clearing, in the endless expanse of shadows, something or someone, watched.

Chapter Twenty-Two

The fire crackled and danced, throwing shadows across the clearing as Sofia shifted closer to the box she'd carried back from the car. The night pressed in around them, the sounds of the forest muted, as if it too were holding its breath.

Iris's gaze flitted nervously between the box and the treeline, but she said nothing.

Sofia hesitated, her fingers hovering over the edges of the lid. "Iris," she began, her voice low, almost reverent, "what I'm about to show you might be hard to process. But I think it's something you need to see."

Iris tilted her head, her brow furrowing. "What's in there?"

Sofia didn't answer immediately. Instead, she slowly lifted the lid, revealing a neat stack of canvases, their edges worn as if they had been handled many times. The faint smell of turpentine and oil paint wafted into the air, mingling with the earthy scent of the forest.

In The Shadow of Perfection

"Here!" Sofia said, pulling out the first canvas, "These are yours."

Iris stared, her expression a mixture of confusion and disbelief. "Mine? What do you mean?"

"You painted these," Sofia said softly. "I found them at your house while you were in the hospital. They were hidden in your studio."

Iris's hand trembled as she reached out to touch the edge of the canvas. "They look like my work, but I don't remember painting anything like this."

Sofia set the canvas in Iris's lap. Iris's breath caught. Edenvale stared back at her, but not the town she knew.

The streets were deserted, the houses bent at strange, impossible angles. Trees stood stripped bare. The whole scene looked sick and twisted, like Edenvale's perfect face had been ripped away to reveal something rotten underneath.

"I don't understand," Iris whispered, her voice barely audible. "Why does it look like this?"

Sofia pulled out the next canvas, handling it like glass. The town square. But not the one they knew. The fountain was split down the middle, its water thick and black. Figures lingered in the shadows, shapeless, watching.

"They look like nightmares," Iris whispered, her fingertips grazing the dried paint. "Why would I paint this?"

"Maybe they're not nightmares," Sofia said carefully. "Maybe they're memories. Or warnings."

Iris's head jerked up. Her eyes locked on Sofia, wide and afraid. "Memories? What are you saying?"

Sofia hesitated, then drew out the next canvas. A white, clinical room. People in lab coats sat around a long table, their faces blurred, bodies stiff. In the background, a screen showed an aerial view of Edenvale. The streets and houses were mapped with meticulous care.

"Does this look familiar to you?" Sofia asked, holding it up so the firelight caught every detail.

Iris froze. "It's the lab. The one from my dreams."

Sofia's mouth tightened. "I don't think they're just dreams, Iris. I think you're remembering something that actually happened. Something they've been trying to erase."

In The Shadow of Perfection

Iris shook her head, fingers gripping the edge of the canvas as if it might keep her steady. "But why? Why would I remember a lab? Why this? What is the connection?"

Sofia reached for another canvas, this one even darker. Rows of Shinies lined the walls of a room, their reflective surfaces catching an artificial light. Beneath each mirror were names, charts, and lines of text that seemed to pulse with an unsettling energy. In the center of the room stood a figure—a woman with her back to the viewer, staring into one of the mirrors.

"This one," Sofia said, placing it beside Iris, "feels like a piece of the puzzle."

Iris leaned closer, her eyes narrowing. "That's me," she said, her voice trembling. "I am pretty sure this is me."

Sofia pulled out another canvas. This one showed Iris, but not the Iris Edenvale adored.

She wore a white lab coat. Her face was hard, her hands gripping a tablet crammed with numbers and graphs. Around her stood others in the same coats, their features blurred, half-recognizable but impossible to place. All except one. Dr. Reynolds. He stood right beside her.

In The Shadow of Perfection

"Do you see this?" Sofia asked, pointing at the tablet drawn on the canvas. "Look closer."

Iris squinted her eyes, her stomach knotting. Reynolds's expression was the same—calm, cold, calculating. His eyes fixed on the tablet like a hawk circling prey.

On the bottom of the canvas, words burned through the firelight in a shade of crimson she never used—like a warning written in blood: *Edenvale Behavioral Rehabilitation Project*. And beneath it, in stark black letters: *Subject IR-105*.

"Iris," Sofia whispered, her voice trembling. "It seems like you were part of this Project. Perhaps you even created it."

Iris recoiled. Her stomach lurched, bile rising in her throat. For a moment she thought she might vomit into the fire. "No. That's not possible. I wouldn't... I couldn't... I don't even know what this is."

Sofia reached for her hand, grounding her. "I know this is overwhelming. But think about everything you've been dreaming, everything you've been remembering. It all points to something bigger. Something they don't want you to know. Something Reynolds doesn't want you to know."

In The Shadow of Perfection

The fire crackled, embers flaring like weak stars against the dark. The forest pressed in, its shadows shifting as if they'd been listening all along.

"I need time," Iris said at last, her voice raw. "I need to make sense of this."

Sofia nodded, though her mind was already racing. "We will. But we have to be careful. If they're watching, if they're listening, we can't let them know we're on to them."

Iris met her eyes. "Then we keep up the act. We pretend everything's normal."

Sofia's smile was thin, brittle. "Exactly. We'll play their game. But on our terms."

As they carefully packed the canvases back into the box, the weight of their discovery hung heavy between them. The fire burned low, its light casting long shadows that seemed to stretch endlessly into the night. Somewhere in the distance, a branch snapped, the sound startling in the stillness.

Both women froze, their eyes darting to the darkened woods. But the forest remained silent, as if holding its breath.

In The Shadow of Perfection

Sofia reached for the box, clutching it tightly. "Let's keep this close. We don't know who or what might be out there." Her fingers dug into the box until the cardboard crumpled, her calm voice a shade too tight.

Iris nodded, her jaw tightening. She sat cross-legged near the flames, her hands fidgeting with the edge of her jacket as though anchoring herself to the present moment.

"Sofia," Iris began hesitantly, her voice barely above a whisper, "there's one more thing; it's about those dreams. There's one that didn't make sense until now. I told you I brought notes. I wrote down what I could remember."

Sofia scooted closer, her expression serious. "Go on."

Taking a deep breath, Iris began. "It starts in a bright, white room. The walls, the floor—everything is sterile. There are machines everywhere, humming softly, and the air feels... heavy. Like it's pressing down on me."

Sofia leaned forward, her hands clasped in front of her. "What else? Who's there?"

"There's a desk," Iris continued, her voice trembling slightly. "It's cluttered with files, thick ones with strange titles. And on the front of one of them, in bold letters, is *Cognitive Reconstruction Trials: Subject IR-105.*"

In The Shadow of Perfection

Sofia's brow furrowed. "Subject IR-105? That's... you?"

Iris nodded slowly. "I think so. The file felt personal somehow, like it held pieces of me. But I didn't get to read much because there was a man there. He spoke to me."

Sofia's breath hitched. "Was it Dr. Reynolds?"

"No," Iris said, shaking her head. "It was someone else. His voice was familiar, but I couldn't place it. He called me by my name, my full name. He said, "Iris, you're pushing yourself too hard. You've been at this for weeks." Yes, that's exactly what he said!" Iris exclaimed.

Sofia's eyes narrowed. "At what? Did he say what you were doing?"

Iris closed her eyes, willing the fragments of the dream to come into focus. "I was working on something called the *Eden Project*. I remember telling him that if it worked, it could redefine how trauma is treated. I said we could rebuild lives, give people a second chance."

Sofia's stomach churned. "Rebuild lives? How? What did he say to that?"

"He pushed back," Iris said, her voice cracking. "He said something about the cost, about the disorientation, and the memory gaps. He asked if it was worth it."

In The Shadow of Perfection

Sofia's face darkened. "And what did you say?"

Iris's lips trembled. "I told him it was worth it. That a life without pain and grief was worth anything."

For a moment, the two women sat in stunned silence, the weight of Iris's words hanging heavy in the air. The fire crackled softly, its warmth doing little to dispel the chill that had settled between them.

Sofia finally broke the silence. "Iris... that doesn't sound like a dream. It sounds like a memory."

Iris looked up at her, her eyes glassy. "I thought so too. But why would I have a memory like that? Why would I have been involved in something like the Eden Project?"

Sofia leaned closer, her voice urgent. "Do you remember anything else? The man?"

Iris's gaze dropped to her hands. "Yes. His name is Dr. Elias Corwin."

Sofia gasped softly. "That name again. Iris, who is he? Do you know him?"

Iris shook her head. "Not really. I mean, I don't think I've ever met him. But in the dream, it felt like I knew him. It felt like I had known him for a long time."

In The Shadow of Perfection

Sofia exhaled slowly, her mind racing. "And you're sure this isn't something you imagined? Something from a book or a movie?"

Iris's voice was firm. "No. It was too vivid. Too specific. And it felt... real, Sofia. More real than the accident."

Reaching into her bag, Iris pulled out a small, worn notebook. The leather cover was scratched, and the pages were filled with hurried handwriting and rough sketches. She opened it to the middle and handed it to Sofia.

"I started writing down what I could remember," Iris said. "It's all jumbled, but maybe you can make sense of it."

Sofia took the notebook, her fingers grazing the edge of the pages. The first entry was scrawled in jagged letters: *White room. Machines. The Eden Project. IR-105. Memory gaps. Second chance.*

She flipped to another page, which held a sketch of what looked like a floor plan. "What's this?" she asked, holding it up.

"I think it's the lab," Iris said. "It came to me in another dream. I don't know how, but I'm sure that's what it is."

Sofia studied the sketch, her pulse quickening. "These look like holding areas. And this," she pointed to a larger space marked with an X, "this could be a central hub. Like a command center."

Iris nodded. "That's what it felt like. And there was a screen. It showed Edenvale. Every street, every house. It was like they were watching everything."

Sofia's breath caught. "Watching... like Shiny?"

Iris's eyes widened. "Maybe. Or something bigger. Something that controls Shiny."

The two women exchanged a long, heavy look, the enormity of their discovery pressing down on them.

"What if Edenvale isn't real?" Sofia whispered, her voice trembling. "What if it's all... part of this Project?"

Iris's chest tightened. "If that's true, then what does that make us? Are we a part of it too?"

The fire crackled louder, a log shifting as sparks flew into the night sky. The world around them felt suddenly too big, too unknown.

Sofia closed the notebook and handed it back to Iris. "We'll figure this out. But we have to be smart. If anyone's watching, we can't let them know we're onto something."

In The Shadow of Perfection

Iris nodded, though fear flickered in her eyes. "We'll play the part. Just like you said. But Sofia... what if they already know?"

Sofia didn't have an answer. She simply placed a reassuring hand on Iris's arm and stared into the fire, her mind churning with questions that felt too dangerous to ask.

Chapter Twenty-Three

Iris and Sofia sat in silence, the weight of their earlier words pressing down, too heavy to name. Even the forest seemed to sense it. The trees stood still, their branches rigid, the night air holding its breath.

Sofia rose, stretching as if to shake it off. "We should call it a night," she said, her tone forced, her gaze flicking nervously to the black line of trees. "We'll need the energy for tomorrow."

Iris pushed herself to her feet, slower, reluctant. Her eyes lingered on the box of canvases, the grotesque shapes burned into her mind. A shiver worked through her. "Yes," she said quietly. "Rest."

They turned toward the tent. That's when it came, a faint rustle, so soft it might have been imagined. Both women froze.

Sofia spun back, scanning the treeline. Her voice dropped to a whisper. "We're not alone."

In The Shadow of Perfection

Iris nodded, her breath catching in her throat, but she quickly shook it off. "It's probably just an animal," she said.

Another rustle. Closer this time. Then, the unmistakable sound of a footstep breaking a twig.

"That's not an animal," Sofia said, her voice tight.

They both stared into the shadows, the firelight casting flickering shapes onto the surrounding trees. And then they saw it—a figure, half-hidden in the darkness, just beyond the reach of the fire's glow.

"Who's there?" Sofia demanded, her voice sharper than she intended.

The figure didn't move. For a long, excruciating moment, the silence stretched between them, thick and suffocating. Then, slowly, the figure stepped forward into the light.

The man was tall, his frame lean but solid, and his face, though lined with faint shadows, was immediately familiar to Iris. Her breath hitched as she took a step back, her hand clutching Sofia's arm for support.

"It's him," Iris whispered, her voice trembling. "The man from my dream."

Sofia's eyes widened. "Which one? The family?"

In The Shadow of Perfection

Iris shook her head, her gaze locked on the man. "No. The lab. He's the doctor. Dr. Elias Corwin."

At the mention of his name, the man inclined his head slightly, his expression calm but unreadable. "You remember," he said, his voice low and even.

Sofia instinctively stepped in front of Iris, her body tense. "Who are you? What do you want?"

Elias raised his hands in a gesture of peace. "I'm not here to harm you," he said. "I'm here to help."

"Help?" Sofia's voice was sharp, almost accusatory. "Help with what? And how did you find us out here?"

Elias hesitated, his gaze flicking between the two women. "There's a lot you don't understand," he said carefully. "But you need to know the truth."

"The truth?" Iris's voice broke, a mix of fear and anger. "The truth about what? About Edenvale? About me?"

"Yes," Elias said simply. "About all of it."

Sofia crossed her arms, her voice low and sharp. "Start with Edenvale. What is it?"

Elias's eyes flicked to the treeline, then back to her. He hesitated, his jaw tightening. "It's... not what it seems."

In The Shadow of Perfection

"That's not good enough," Sofia snapped. She took a step closer, her body taut with suspicion. "What is it?"

His lips pressed into a line before he finally spoke. "It's a controlled environment. A test. A study of life without pain, without grief."

Iris's stomach turned. The words landed like blows. "A test?" she whispered. "On us?"

Elias didn't answer. His silence was damning.

Sofia's voice cut through the night like glass. "Say it."

"Yes," he admitted at last, his voice low. "On you. It's a test on everyone here. It's a Project."

"So what about this Project? What does it do exactly?" Sofia's eyes narrowed.

"Edenvale is exactly what it sounds like. Eden and a veil. A paradise to live in, a veil to cover everything you grieved and all the painful memories related to your life before," said Elias.

"So, this whole town is a Project?" Sofia asked.

"It isn't just a town. It's a controlled experiment, built to test what happens when people live without pain, without grief. A life polished, perfected, engineered to look flawless," Elias continued.

In The Shadow of Perfection

Sofia stared at him, her jaw tightening. "Engineered? You mean... everything about Edenvale is fake?"

Elias nodded. "In a sense, yes. The town, the people... even the memories of those who live in Edenvale. They've all been carefully curated. They are real people, of course. But their lives and experiences have been altered."

Iris's heart pounded in her chest. "What do you mean their lives and memories were altered? What about me? What about my life and memories?"

Elias met her gaze, his expression somber. "You had a life before Edenvale, Iris. A life you chose to leave behind."

Iris stumbled back a step, shaking her head. "That doesn't make sense. Why would I be part of something like this?"

Elias hesitated again. His gaze lingered on her, heavy, almost mournful. "Because you chose to be."

Iris's pulse roared in her ears. "Chose?" Her voice cracked. "You're saying I agreed to this?"

"You begged for it," he said, his tone almost breaking. "You asked to forget."

In The Shadow of Perfection

The fire popped, sparks bursting into the air. For a long moment, no one moved.

Finally, Iris's voice tore through the silence, ragged. "Why would I do that? Why would I ask to forget?"

"Because you were in pain," Elias said, his tone heavy with regret. "You experienced something so devastating that you volunteered to become part of the Eden Project. It was a chance to start over, to live without the weight of your past."

Sofia's eyes blazed. "And who gave you the right to strip her of her memories?"

"She did. It was her own choice," Elias said firmly. "Iris knew what she was agreeing to. She was warned she was going to forget everything else as if it never happened. But she didn't know everything. None of you did."

"What is it that we don't know?" Iris demanded, her voice rising.

Elias hesitated, his jaw tightening. "The Project wasn't supposed to be permanent. It was meant to be a temporary escape, a way to heal. But something changed. The people funding the Project and controlling it had other plans."

In The Shadow of Perfection

"What kind of plans?" Sofia pressed.

Elias shook his head. "I can't tell you that. Not yet."

Sofia took a step forward, her hands clenched into fists. "Why not? If you're really here to help us, you'll tell us everything."

"Wait! Who is running this Project?" Iris asked.

Elias's gaze softened. "If I tell you too much now, you'll be in even greater danger. The people running this... they're watching. Always. And if they suspect you know the truth, they'll erase everything."

Iris's breath hitched. "Erase? You mean... my memories?"

"And more," Elias said grimly. "You're not just a participant anymore, Iris. You're a threat. Both of you are."

Sofia's voice trembled with anger. "Then why are you here? If you're not going to give us answers, why come at all?"

"To warn you," Elias said. "And to help you prepare. You'll need to move carefully. Gather information. Trust no one."

In The Shadow of Perfection

"You sound just like Shiny," Iris whispered.

"In a way," he said quietly, "I am Shiny."

Sofia blinked, her voice cutting through the firelight. "What are you talking about?"

"When you received Shiny at your doors," he said, "your Shiny and all the rest of the devices were designed to observe and listen. I cracked the code to your Shiny, Iris. It was the only way I could reach you from the outside. The only way I could try to help."

"Help?" Iris's voice rose, trembling. "You nearly drove me insane!"

His expression hardened. "I didn't have full control over the device. But it was the only way to jolt your memories awake, to prepare you for what's coming. I needed you to remember, Iris. I needed you to wake up."

The fire crackled loudly in the silence that followed, its light casting strange shadows on Elias's face. Iris stared at him, her mind racing with questions she couldn't bring herself to ask.

"Why should we trust you?" Sofia finally asked, her voice low and dangerous.

Elias's expression softened. "Because I'm the one who put you in Edenvale, Iris. I was standing right next to you before you departed. I pleaded with you not to go. I asked you if you were sure about it. And now I'm the one trying to get you out."

The words hung in the air. Iris sank to the ground, her hands trembling.

Sofia stepped in front of her, her body rigid with tension. "You'd better not be lying," she said, her voice ice-cold. "Because if you are, I swear..."

"Sofia, it's okay!" Iris interrupted as she stood up. "Who is running the Project? You still haven't answered."

"Sofia, I'm not lying," Elias said, his voice steady. "But there's more you need to know. You were never supposed to be here as a participant, Iris. This Project is yours. It was all your idea. You were the mastermind. I can't tell you who is running it, though."

Iris froze, her breath catching. "My idea? What are you talking about?"

"You were one of us," Elias said, his tone tinged with regret. "A brilliant scientist, a leader in behavioral sciences. You had been studying human behavior and how it relates to happiness. The topic fascinated you. You wished to discover what the true things are that make us happy. You wanted to know whether we could ever be truly happy when everything was perfect, ordinary, and predictable. You designed the Eden Project. You conceived it, nurtured it, and believed in its promise."

Iris shook her head vehemently, her body stiffening as if the very words were a physical blow. She took a step back, her hands trembling. "No. That's not possible. Why would I create something like this?"

Elias stepped forward cautiously, his voice tinged with an earnest desperation. "Because you wanted to help people, Iris. You saw their pain—the kind of pain that strips away hope, that makes life unbearable. The Project was everything you dreamed it would be at first—a chance to give people a life free from grief, from loss, from suffering. It was never meant to be like this. It was supposed to be a temporary experience, a way to heal, to help people find new meaning."

Sofia interjected, her voice sharp with suspicion. "Then what changed? If this was her Project, why is she here now? Why doesn't she remember any of it?"

Elias hesitated, his expression clouding with something unreadable. He looked at Iris, his gaze heavy with an emotion she couldn't quite name. "Because you chose to forget," he said finally, his words slow and deliberate. "After what happened."

In The Shadow of Perfection

"What happened?" Iris demanded, her voice cracking under the weight of her own desperation. "What was so terrible that I'd erase my own memory?"

Elias's jaw tightened, and he glanced away as if the answer were a burden he could barely carry. For a moment, it seemed he might refuse to speak. Then, with a strained voice, he said, "You lost everything. Your family, Iris. Your entire world shattered, and you couldn't see another way forward. That's when you made the choice. You became the first and the only fully vested participant from our team. The first scientist to experience the Project from the inside. You stepped into the world you created."

Iris pressed a trembling hand to her mouth. Her voice came out in a broken whisper. "The family I've been dreaming of... and painting. Are they my family?"

Elias hesitated, his face taut with pain. "They were."

Chapter Twenty-Four

Iris's breath hitched, and she stumbled back a step, as though the truth itself were pulling her down. "I see glimpses of them in my dreams, but I don't remember them—not really. I don't remember my life. I don't remember how I lost them."

"That's the point," Elias said, his voice thick with regret. "The Eden Project was meant to be a sanctuary, a chance to start again. It was for people who'd hit rock bottom, who saw no way out. You gave them hope, Iris. You gave them this place. But then you joined them, and everything... changed."

Sofia's eyes narrowed, her mind racing. "Dr. Reynolds," she said, her tone low and accusatory. "It was him, wasn't it? He is the one running the Project, right?"

Elias nodded grimly. "He took over after Iris entered the program. At first, he seemed aligned with the mission— refining the process and ensuring its success. But over time, his motives shifted. He wanted control. Absolute control. And now..." Elias's voice faltered, and for a moment, he seemed haunted by the weight of his own words. "Now he's steering the Project toward something dangerous."

"What do you mean, 'dangerous'?" Sofia asked, her suspicion sharpening into fear.

Elias's gaze darted to the shadows surrounding them, his posture tense, as if expecting something or someone to emerge. He lowered his voice. "People have started to remember, like Iris has. At first, it's fragments—little things that don't make sense. But as they dig deeper, the memories come back. And when they do..."

Sofia leaned forward, her fists clenching. "What happens to them?"

"They disappear," Elias said, his voice barely audible. "Not just from Edenvale. They vanish completely. No trace. No explanation. It's as if they never existed."

Iris stared at him, her mind spinning. "Why? Why would anyone do this?"

"To protect the Project," Elias replied, his tone laced with bitterness. "Or at least, that's what Reynolds tells himself. Of course, he doesn't know I have figured it out. Anyone who threatens the illusion, anyone who starts to pull at the seams, becomes a liability. And Reynolds doesn't tolerate liabilities."

Sofia's breath quickened. "So what about us? Right now? Does talking about this make us liabilities?"

Elias's expression darkened, his gaze fixed on the flickering flames between them. "Not yet. But the more you uncover, the closer you'll get to the line. That's why I came. I came to warn you. To help you."

"Help us?" Iris asked, her voice shaking with skepticism. "How? How can you help us when you were part of this?"

Elias's face hardened. "I was part of it, but not anymore. I stayed because I thought I could fix it from the inside. But Reynolds..." He exhaled, his voice heavy with resignation. "Reynolds has turned it into something else entirely. He's rewriting the rules, and the cost is too high. People are vanishing, and I don't know how to end this. But I have to stop it."

Sofia's eyes burned into him. "Why now, Elias? Why didn't you do something earlier?"

"I didn't know how far he'd go," Elias admitted. "Also, I didn't want to lose access to the Project. It was my way of ensuring Iris was still okay. But now, it's clear. The only way to stop this is to tear it down. Completely. And for that, I need your help."

Sofia narrowed her eyes. "I don't know if we can trust you."

Elias met her gaze steadily. "You don't have to. But you need the truth, and I'm the only one who is willing to give it to you."

The fire crackled, flames rising into the air, but its warmth couldn't touch the icy tension. Elias's words sliced through the silence. Disbelief, anger, and a gnawing grief tore at Iris all at once, a storm she couldn't contain.

"If all of this is true," she finally managed, her voice trembling with the weight of her question, "then what happens now? What do we do?"

Elias fixed her with a steady gaze, his expression resolute but edged with a hint of desperation. "We uncover the truth. Piece by piece. Together."

Sofia interjected. "Wait, you talked about all those people—the broken ones, the ones with nothing left. Am I one of them? Why am I part of the Eden Project? What happened to me?" The words burst out of her like a dam breaking, her voice echoing against the trees.

In The Shadow of Perfection

Before Elias could respond, the faint snap of a twig echoed through the still night, cutting through the tension like a knife. The three froze. Elias's head jerked toward the sound, his eyes narrowing as his body tensed.

"Stay quiet," he murmured, his voice barely audible. "There's someone here."

Chapter Twenty-Five

The clearing plunged into an oppressive silence, the kind that seemed to magnify every small sound. The soft rustle of leaves in the breeze now felt menacing, the shadows pressing in like silent witnesses. Iris's heart pounded, her chest tight with dread. Without thinking, she reached for Sofia's hand, gripping it tightly as if to ground herself.

Then another sound—a crunch of footsteps, heavier this time, closer.

"Who's there?" Sofia's voice wavered, but she forced a note of defiance into her words.

No answer.

Elias stepped closer to the fire, his stance protective, his movements deliberate. "Get behind me," he said quietly, his gaze locked on the dark treeline.

In The Shadow of Perfection

The footsteps grew louder, each one measured and slow. Then a shadow emerged, shifting just beyond the firelight.

"Perhaps your husband can explain what happened to you, Sofia, and how you ended up in Edenvale," Elias murmured, his tone biting, his eyes fixed on the approaching figure.

Iris felt a chill sweep over her as the figure stepped into the firelight. Sofia let out a soft gasp, her breath hitching. Mark stood before them, his expression unreadable, but the glint in his eyes sent a shiver down Iris's spine.

"Mark?" Sofia's voice was a strained whisper. "What... what are you doing here?"

Mark's lips curved into a small, cynical smile. "I think you've asked enough questions for one night, don't you, sweetheart?" His tone condescending, his words as sharp as the cold night air. He looked at Elias, his jaw tightening. "Quite the unexpected gathering, isn't it? Mind if I join you? You know, Dr. Corwin, my father won't be pleased about this. We had an agreement."

"Your father?" Sofia echoed, her confusion palpable. "Mark, what are you talking about? You said your father had died when you were little."

In The Shadow of Perfection

"No, Sofia, Mark's father is very much alive." Elias said, his voice laced with bitterness. "Of course, he can't play the role of his father in Edenvale."

"Who is it? Who is his father?" Sofia asked.

"Mark's father is the person who is in control of all this. Even in control of you, Sofia," Elias said bitterly.

Mark's eyes flick to Elias instead of answering.

"Reynolds!" Sofia gasped.

"Bingo!" exclaimed Elias.

Sofia's head whipped toward Mark, disbelief etched across her face. "You knew about all of this? You were part of it? Who even are you?"

Mark's eyes never left Elias. "Why are you doing this?" His tone darkened, a dangerous edge creeping in. "You're sabotaging my father's life's work, trying to tear down something bigger than you could ever understand."

Elias's jaw clenched. "The Project has changed, Mark. Your father has changed. You were never a fully vested member, and, of course, your father wouldn't share his true intentions with you. Because if you knew what was truly happening, you would be the first one to try and stop him. You don't see it now, but..."

In The Shadow of Perfection

"No!" Mark snapped, his voice cutting through the air. "The only thing that's changed is your jealousy, Elias. You couldn't handle the fact that my father took over. You are still resentful because you didn't get to carry the torch. You thought when Dr. Iris Valen stepped down, the Project would be yours. But guess what? You were wrong. And now you're trying to destroy it out of jealousy."

"This isn't jealousy," Elias countered, his tone sharp with conviction. "This is about protecting people. Do you even know what your father's been doing? The disappearances, the experiments?"

Mark's eyes narrowed. "What disappearances? What experiments? Stop spinning your lies."

Elias's voice grew colder. "Go ahead. Try to find the people who have vanished from Edenvale. You won't. There's no trace of them because your father made sure of it. He has turned this place into a cage, and he is the one holding the key."

Mark's face darkened. "You're lying."

"Am I?" Elias challenged. "The files I've seen, the plans I've read, they're not about healing or happiness. They're about control. About pushing boundaries, no matter the cost. Natural disasters. Fabricated crises.

In The Shadow of Perfection

Freak accidents. Testing human behavior in ways no one consented to."

"That's insane," Mark said, though his voice faltered.

"Actually, it's not just insane; it's also immoral and illegal. But it is happening." Elias shot back. "This isn't what Iris envisioned. This isn't what we all signed up for. It's become something monstrous."

Sofia's voice broke through the tension, trembling with uncertainty. "Is it true, Mark? Is he telling the truth?"

Mark hesitated, his jaw tightening. "You don't understand. This is bigger than us. It is bigger than anyone here. My father is doing what's necessary to ensure the success of the Project."

Elias stepped closer, his voice low but cutting. "At what cost, Mark? How many lives will it take before you realize he's gone too far?"

Mark looked away, his face a mask of conflict. For a moment, the only sound was the whisper of the wind through the trees. And then he spoke, his voice barely audible. "You're wrong about my father. He's doing what needs to be done. But... I'll find out for myself."

Elias and Sofia exchanged a tense glance as Mark turned and started walking toward the shadows.

In The Shadow of Perfection

"For the sake of the friendship we once had, we need your help," Elias yelled after him. "I have proof of everything I am saying. Mark, please!" Mark stopped in his tracks.

Chapter Twenty-Six

The morning in Edenvale was deceptively serene. The air carried the faint sweetness of flowers, and the streets were impeccably clean, as if the world itself had conspired to maintain the illusion of perfection. Yet within the walls of Sofia's home, the atmosphere was anything but tranquil. The curtains were drawn tight to keep curious eyes from peeking inside

Sofia sat at her dining table, her fingers tapping nervously against the wood. Mark was pacing the length of the room, his face a mask of conflict. Across from Sofia, Iris sat with her hands clasped tightly together, her knuckles white against her skin. Elias leaned against the doorway, his posture calm but his eyes alert, watching Mark like a predator sizing up its prey.

"So, let me get this straight," Mark said, breaking the silence. His voice was low, measured, but there was an edge to it. "You want me to go against my own father? To expose everything he's worked for?"

In The Shadow of Perfection

"No," Elias said evenly. "We're asking you to help us expose the truth. There's a difference."

Mark stopped pacing and turned to face him. "And what happens when this all blows up in our faces? When he finds out what we're doing?"

Sofia interjected, her voice firm. "Mark, people are vanishing. Do you even know what happens to them?"

Mark's jaw tightened. "No. I don't."

"That's exactly the problem," Sofia said, leaning forward. "None of us do. And if we don't act, we could be next."

Iris's voice was quieter, almost hesitant, but it carried an undercurrent of steel. "This was never supposed to happen. The Eden Project was meant to help people, not erase them. If we don't stop this, it's only going to get worse."

Mark ran a hand through his hair, his shoulders sagging. "You don't know my father. He doesn't lose. He doesn't forgive."

Elias stepped forward, his voice firm but not unkind. "Then we don't let him know we're onto him. Not yet. We play the part—perfect citizens, perfect lives. But behind the scenes, we gather evidence, piece by piece."

In The Shadow of Perfection

Sofia nodded. "We don't have to take him down all at once. We just need to start uncovering the truth."

Mark hesitated, his gaze flicking between them. Finally, he sighed. "All right. I'm in. But if we do this, we do it carefully. If he suspects anything..."

Elias nodded. "He won't. Not if we're smart."

The four exchanged tense glances, the enormity of their task settling over them like a heavy fog.

The next few days were a study in duality. By day, the four played their roles as model citizens of Edenvale. Mark accompanied Sofia to neighborhood gatherings, their smiles fixed and conversations light. Iris returned to her painting, creating bright, cheerful scenes that masked the turmoil inside her. Elias, ever the outsider, maintained a low profile, slipping in and out of town unnoticed.

But at night, their facade cracked. They met in secret, poring over documents Elias had smuggled out of the lab and comparing notes on the town's growing anomalies.

"I've been watching the Shinies," Sofia said one evening, her voice hushed. "Mine started saying things that don't make sense. Compliments, yes, but also... warnings. Subtle ones."

In The Shadow of Perfection

"Like what?" Iris asked, leaning forward.

"'Stay within the light,'" Sofia replied. "And once, it said, 'Deviation is dangerous.'"

Elias frowned. "They're programmed to monitor behavior. Anything outside the parameters of perfection could trigger a response."

Mark, who had been silent, spoke up. "That's not all. I looked through some of my father's files. There's a list of the people who've disappeared."

Sofia's eyes widened. "Do you know where they went?"

Mark shook his head. "No. Just dates when they vanished. But it gets worse. Some of them... they're marked as 'recalibrated.' I don't know what that means, but it doesn't sound good."

"Recalibrated?" Iris whispered, her stomach twisting at the word. "Are they being experimented on?"

"Possibly," Elias said, his voice grim. "Or worse."

As the days passed, they began to notice subtle changes in Edenvale. A neighbor, Mrs. Haverly, who had always been the epitome of cheer, suddenly stopped attending community events. Her garden, once the envy of the block, wilted overnight. When Sofia tried to visit, the door was answered by a man in a suit who simply said, "She's resting."

At the grocery store, Iris overheard two women whispering about how the Shinies had started glitching. "Mine told me to stay inside today," one of them said, her voice trembling. "It's never done that before."

"Mine, too," the other replied. "It said something about preserving order."

The unease spread like a shadow across the town, but no one dared speak of it openly.

One evening, the four met in Sofia's garage, a safe distance from prying eyes. Mark brought a folder he'd stolen from his father's office, its contents filled with cryptic charts and diagrams.

"This," he said, pointing to a chart, "is a timeline. It shows how the Eden Project was supposed to evolve. But these changes here,"— he tapped the paper— "they don't match the original plan."

"What do they mean?" Iris asked, her voice trembling.

Mark hesitated. "I don't know. But I think they're tied to the disappearances."

In The Shadow of Perfection

Before anyone could respond, the garage light flickered. A low hum filled the air, followed by the unmistakable sound of a car pulling into the driveway.

Sofia's breath caught. "Who is that?"

Mark's face paled. "It's him."

Chapter Twenty-Seven

The garage door began to creak open, revealing the dark silhouette of Dr. Reynolds standing in the doorway.

"Well," he said, his voice calm but menacing, "I see you've been busy."

The four froze, the weight of Dr. Reynolds's presence paralyzing them. The fluorescent garage light flickered again, casting eerie shadows across his figure. He stepped forward with deliberate slowness, the sound of his polished shoes on the concrete unnaturally loud in the silence.

Mark recovered first, stepping in front of Sofia and squaring his shoulders. "Dad, what are you doing here?"

Dr. Reynolds tilted his head slightly, his expression unreadable. "I might ask you the same, son. Late-night meetings in garages aren't typically part of Edenvale's charming routines, are they? And Sofia? You don't seem surprised to have discovered that I am your father-in-law."

195

In The Shadow of Perfection

Sofia's pulse raced. She felt Iris inch closer to her, their mutual fear unspoken but palpable. Elias, standing slightly apart, kept his eyes trained on Dr. Reynolds, his body tense like a coiled spring.

"We were just catching up," Mark said, his tone carefully neutral. "Iris hasn't been well, and we thought a little company would do her good."

Dr. Reynolds's gaze slid to Iris, his sharp eyes assessing her. "Ah, yes. Our recovering artist. How are you feeling, Iris? Settling back into your routine, I hope?"

Iris forced a weak smile, her voice trembling slightly. "Yes, thank you. Everything is... back to normal."

Dr. Reynolds's lips twitched into what might have been a smile, though it lacked warmth. "Normal is good. It's the foundation of Edenvale, after all. We wouldn't want anything disrupting that."

Elias took a step forward, his voice calm but firm. "Why are you here, Dr. Reynolds?"

Reynolds's gaze flicked to him, and his expression hardened. "And here we have the prodigal doctor. Still lurking where you don't belong, I see."

Elias didn't flinch. "I could say the same about you."

In The Shadow of Perfection

A charged silence fell over the group, the tension crackling like static electricity. Sofia could feel the weight of Reynolds's authority bearing down on them, his presence suffocating.

"You know," Reynolds said, breaking the silence, "Edenvale is built on trust. Trust in the system, trust in each other. When that trust erodes... well, things can unravel quickly."

Mark stepped forward, his jaw clenched. "We're not eroding anything. We're just talking."

Dr. Reynolds's gaze lingered on his son, a flicker of something unspoken passing between them. "Be careful, Mark. Conversations have consequences."

"What kind of consequences?" Mark asked, his voice edged with defiance.

Reynolds didn't answer immediately. Instead, he looked around the garage, his eyes landing on the folder still open on the table. His expression darkened.

"Where did you get that?" he asked, his voice dangerously soft.

Mark's throat tightened. "It doesn't matter."

In The Shadow of Perfection

Dr. Reynolds stepped closer, his presence looming. "It matters. That information is classified, Mark. It's not meant for unsanctioned eyes."

"It wasn't meant for lies, either," Elias said sharply. "Or disappearances."

Reynolds's attention snapped to Elias, his calm facade cracking for the first time. "You don't know what you're talking about."

"I know enough," Elias countered. "I know about the experiments, the people you've erased. How long do you think you can keep this charade going?"

Sofia's breath caught. This was the confrontation they'd all been dreading, and yet the one they couldn't avoid.

Reynolds's face hardened, his voice dropping to a chilling whisper. "You think you're uncovering the truth? You're children playing with fire. You have no idea what you're up against."

"Then tell us," Sofia said, surprising herself with the steadiness of her voice. "If we're so wrong, why don't you tell us the truth?"

Reynolds looked at her, his eyes cold and unyielding. "The truth is dangerous. And some things are better left buried."

In The Shadow of Perfection

The room fell silent, the weight of his words suffocating. But before anyone could respond, the faint sound of a car engine echoed in the distance. Reynolds's head tilted slightly, his demeanor shifting.

"I've said enough," he said, stepping back toward the garage door. "But let this be a warning. Stop digging. For your own sake."

He turned and disappeared into the night, leaving the group in stunned silence. The hum of his car faded, and the oppressive quiet of the garage settled over them like a shroud.

Elias broke the silence, his voice low. "He's scared. That's why he came."

Mark ran a hand through his hair, his face pale. "Scared or not, he won't let this go. He'll be watching us now."

Sofia swallowed hard. "Then we need to move faster. We can't wait for him to come after us."

Iris looked at each of them, her resolve hardening. "Then we keep going. We don't stop until we have the truth."

The fire of determination in her eyes was mirrored in the others. They had crossed a line, and there was no turning back now.

Chapter Twenty-Eight

The morning sunlight poured through the gaps in the curtains, casting fractured patterns on the table. The kitchen, like everything in Edenvale, was flawless—pristine counters, perfectly aligned chairs, and an air of order that now felt unsettling. But the atmosphere inside Sofia and Mark's home was anything but peaceful.

Iris sat at the table, cradling her cup of tea as if it were an anchor. Her thoughts were a storm, fragments of memories flashing through her mind like lightning. A family she had loved. A life she couldn't fully recall. The sterile halls of a lab. The voice of Dr. Elias Corwin. The truths she had learned the night before felt impossible to reconcile, but the growing fire in her chest told her she couldn't turn back now.

Elias sat across from her, his posture rigid but his eyes filled with quiet determination. Sofia paced by the window, her arms crossed tightly over her chest. Mark leaned against the counter, his jaw tight, his gaze fixed on the floor. The silence in the room was heavy, pregnant with unspoken fears and simmering tension.

Iris broke the silence first, her voice steady but tinged with vulnerability. "If I created the Eden Project, then I must have believed in it. I must have thought it was something good. But now... I don't even know what to believe."

Elias leaned forward, his voice soft but firm. "You believed in helping people, Iris. That's who you are. That's who you've always been. You wanted to create a place where people could heal, where they could start over after unimaginable loss. And for a time, that's exactly what the Eden Project was. But things changed after Reynolds took full control."

Iris's gaze sharpened. "I came here to forget. To escape the pain of losing my family, right? But if I was the one who started this, then why didn't anyone stop Reynolds from taking over?"

Elias hesitated, his expression darkening. "Reynolds is... persuasive. He convinced everyone that his direction was the logical next step. That the Project needed stricter control, better monitoring. At first, it seemed like he was right. The participants were thriving. But over time, his true intentions became clear."

In The Shadow of Perfection

"What intentions?" Iris pressed, her voice rising slightly.

Elias glanced at Sofia and Mark, then back to Iris. "Control. Absolute control. Reynolds doesn't want to help people heal; he wants to dictate how they live. He's turned Edenvale into a giant experiment, a Petri dish where he can manipulate every variable. This was not part of the agreement. The participants didn't sign up to be lab rats who could be tortured and manipulated. They came willingly to let go of pain and have a new chance at life. What he is about to do to the town of Edenvale is immoral and illegal. Now he's pushing the boundaries more than ever, designing plans for crises and crafting natural disasters. Also, people are starting to remember. And when they do, they disappear. Every trace of them is removed. It's as if they never existed. Reynolds calls it 'maintaining the integrity of the Project.' I call it something else."

Murder. The unspoken word hung in the air like a ghost, and the weight of it made Sofia's stomach turn. She gripped the edge of the counter, her knuckles white. "He is not going to let us continue investigating, is he? We could be next. It wouldn't be hard to make us disappear. Remember, in Edenvale, no one asks questions, no one wonders," she whispered.

In The Shadow of Perfection

Elias's gaze softened. "That's why I'm here. To make things right."

Sofia stared at him for a long moment before her gaze shifted to Mark. Her voice wavered, but her words were firm. "Mark, why did we come here? Why did you bring me to this place?"

Mark's eyes darted to Elias, then back to Sofia. "Sofia, I... I didn't think you'd ever need to know."

Sofia's voice rose, tinged with anger. "Didn't think I'd need to know? I've been living in this illusion, raising children I can't even be sure are mine, and you didn't think I'd need to know?"

Mark's shoulders sagged. "You were in so much pain, Sofia. After the miscarriages, after the..." He broke off, his voice choking on the words.

"Say it," Sofia demanded, her eyes brimming with tears. "After what?"

"After the stillbirth," Mark said softly. "After you tried to end your own life."

Sofia staggered back as if the words had physically struck her. She sank into a chair, her hands trembling. "I don't... I don't remember trying to..." Her voice faltered, and she pressed a hand to her mouth.

In The Shadow of Perfection

"You were broken, Sofia," Mark said, his voice filled with anguish. "And I was terrified. Terrified of losing you. My father told me about the Eden Project, about how it could help people heal. I thought... I thought it was the only way to save you."

Sofia's tears spilled over, but her voice was cold. "And the kids? Emma and Caleb? Are they even ours?"

Mark hesitated, his silence answering the question before he spoke. "They're not. They were children who had lost their families. They had no one to care for them. When we joined the Project, my father said we could take them in, give them a new life. They don't remember their past, Sofia. They think we're their parents."

Sofia's breath hitched, her tears falling freely now. "You decided all of this for me. You took away my opportunity to choose."

"I was trying to protect you," Mark said desperately. "To give you a chance at happiness."

Sofia shook her head, her voice filled with bitterness. "You didn't give me happiness, Mark. You gave me a lie."

Elias intervened, his tone calm but firm. "Sofia, Mark made a terrible mistake, but right now, we need to focus on what comes next. The four of us have a chance to stop Reynolds, to expose the truth about this place. But we have to do it together."

Iris, who had been silent during the exchange, spoke up. "Sofia, I understand your anger. I do. But we can't change the past. What we can do is make sure no one else has to go through what we've been through. We have to end this."

Sofia wiped her eyes, her anger simmering beneath the surface. "Fine. But I'm doing this for Emma and Caleb. They deserve the truth, even if I never get it."

Mark reached for her hand, but she pulled away. He looked at her with pleading eyes, but she refused to meet his gaze.

Elias cleared his throat, his face darkening as he leaned forward. "Reynolds knows," he said grimly. "When he left last night, he wasn't retreating—he was regrouping. He knows we're plotting against him, and he won't sit back and let it happen."

Sofia's hands tightened into fists at her sides. "So, what do we do? He controls everything. The town, the people... even us, in a way. He is holding all the cards!"

Elias shook his head. "No one ever holds all the cards. There's still a chance. But we have to be smart about this. We have to be very careful. If we're going to stop him, we need the people on our side."

Mark frowned. "How are we supposed to do that? These people don't even know they've forgotten their lives. They're happy in their perfect little bubble."

Iris spoke up, her voice quiet but resolute. "Then we have to make them question it. Find cracks in their memories, like the ones I've been seeing in my dreams. If we can plant seeds of doubt, maybe they'll start to remember on their own."

Elias nodded, his expression grim. "It's a start. But there's something else, something we need to deal with first."

He reached into his bag and pulled out a folder, its edges worn and frayed. "These are some of the files I managed to take before I was banned from the lab. Most of it is technical data—records of memory modifications and behavioral studies—but there's something else."

Sofia leaned forward, her brow furrowing. "What is it?"

Elias hesitated, his voice dropping to a near whisper. "A bomb."

In The Shadow of Perfection

The room fell silent, the weight of the word crashing down like a thunderclap. Iris stared at Elias, her face pale. "A bomb? What are you talking about? I never would have agreed to that."

Elias opened the folder, spreading out a series of schematics across the table. "This wasn't part of the original Project. It happened after you left, Iris. It was added much later by someone on the lab team. The files don't name the person directly, but based on the notes, I think I know who it was."

"Who?" Mark asked, his voice sharp.

Elias looked at the papers, then back at them. "Dr. Simon Darnell. He was a friend, a good one. He was the one who first told me something was wrong with the Project, long before I started to see it for myself. But these files... they suggest he built the bomb."

Sofia's eyes widened. "Perhaps he wasn't as good as you thought. Why would he do that?"

Elias's voice was heavy with disbelief. "I don't know. Maybe he was trying to create a fail-safe, a way to destroy Edenvale if things went too far. Or maybe Reynolds forced him into it. Either way, the bomb exists, and if Reynolds gets desperate enough, he could use it."

In The Shadow of Perfection

The words hung in the air like a noose, tightening with each passing second.

"Do we know where it is?" Iris asked, her voice trembling.

Elias shook his head. "No. The schematics don't say. But I know Simon—he would've hidden it somewhere Reynolds couldn't easily reach."

Sofia exhaled sharply, her mind racing. "So we have a ticking time bomb, literally, and a town full of people who don't even know they're being controlled. Great!"

"There's more," Elias said, his voice grim. "The antidote."

Iris's head snapped up. "The antidote?"

"Yes," Elias said, spreading out another set of documents. "The formula for the drug that keeps everyone's memories suppressed—it's stored in the lab. But without access, I can't recreate it. If we could get our hands on it, we could start to wake people up."

Mark frowned. "But how? Reynolds won't just let us waltz into the lab and take it."

Elias's jaw tightened. "No, he won't. But there's a way in. There is an old maintenance corridor that was used during the lab's construction. If we can access it, we might be able to get to the files without triggering the security system."

Sofia nodded, her mind already working through the logistics. "And once we have the antidote? How do we distribute it without raising suspicion?"

Elias hesitated, then glanced at Iris. "That's where you come in."

"Me?" Iris asked, her voice tinged with doubt.

"You're the face of the Eden Project," Elias said. "Even if people don't remember it, they trust you. If we can wake you up completely, restore all your memories, you can help us rally the town. You were the heart of this Project once. You can be it again."

Iris's chest tightened as his words sank in. Memories flickered at the edges of her mind—white lab coats, bustling corridors, the hum of machinery. A voice echoed in her thoughts, her own voice from another life: *"The Eden Project isn't just a sanctuary. It's a lifeline."*

She clenched her fists, her resolve hardening. "We have to stop this. Whatever it takes."

Sofia nodded, her expression fierce. "And we will. But we need to be careful. Reynolds isn't just going to sit back and let us unravel his plans. We have to play the part, act like perfect citizens while we work in the shadows."

Mark, who had been silent, finally spoke. "And if we fail?"

Elias's gaze darkened. "We can't. Too many lives depend on this."

The group exchanged a solemn look, the weight of their mission pressing down on them. As they began to map out their next steps, the enormity of what lay ahead became clear. They weren't just fighting for themselves—they were fighting for the soul of Edenvale.

Chapter Twenty-Nine

The four sat around the dining table in Mark and Sofia's house, their faces illuminated by the faint glow of a single lamp. The curtains were drawn tightly, and every sound outside seemed amplified. The errant gust of wind, the creak of a branch—all reminders that they were living on borrowed time.

Sofia glanced nervously at the Shiny hanging on the far wall, its surface eerily dull. It hadn't emitted its usual compliments or reminders all morning, and the silence unsettled her. "Do you think it's broken?" she asked, her voice barely above a whisper.

Elias studied it for a long moment. "No. I think it's been disabled."

Iris tilted her head. "Disabled? By whom?"

"Dr. Darnell," Elias said confidently. "He built the network that connects all the Shinies to the lab. If they're not working, it means he's done something to disrupt the system."

In The Shadow of Perfection

Mark leaned forward, his hands clasped tightly on the table. "Why would he do that now?"

Elias met his gaze, his expression unreadable. "Because he knows we're planning something. This is his way of saying he's on our side."

The room fell silent as the weight of his words sank in. Finally, Iris spoke. "If that's true, we need to act fast. If Darnell's helping us, it won't be long before Reynolds figures it out."

Elias nodded. "Agreed. Here's what we need to do: First, we have to find the bomb. If Darnell built it, he might have hidden it somewhere Reynolds wouldn't think to look. Second, we need the formula for the antidote or the antidote itself. Without it, we can't wake anyone up. Third, we have to shut off the power to Edenvale. That will sever the connection between the lab and the town, cutting off Reynolds's control."

Sofia frowned. "How are we supposed to do all that without getting caught? Reynolds has eyes everywhere."

"We play the part," Iris said firmly, her voice steady despite the storm brewing inside her. "We smile, we act like everything's fine, and we follow the rules. Meanwhile, we work in the shadows."

In The Shadow of Perfection

Elias tapped the table, drawing their attention. "There's one more problem we need to solve. Every participant in Edenvale has a tracking chip implanted. If anyone gets too close to the town's boundaries, alarms go off. That's why none of you can leave. But I can."

Mark's brow furrowed. "How?"

"I was never implanted," Elias said simply. "I wasn't supposed to stay in Edenvale permanently. My role was to oversee the Project and ensure everything ran smoothly. When I started questioning Reynolds, he cut me off from the lab but never restricted my movements. I guess he overlooked that part. This means I can still come and go as I please, as long as I use my secret paths."

Sofia's eyes lit up. "Then you can contact Darnell. If he's helping us, he might know where the bomb is and how we can access the antidote."

Elias nodded. "That's the plan. I'll leave tonight and try to reach him. But in the meantime, you three need to start sowing seeds of doubt. People are already starting to notice things—changes in themselves, cracks in the town's perfection. You need to encourage them to question what's happening without revealing too much."

In The Shadow of Perfection

Sofia hesitated. "What if they tell Reynolds? After all, everyone still thinks he is just the town's doctor. The one who healed Iris. Many of the townspeople admire and trust him. What if they remain loyal to him and tell him what we are trying to do?"

Elias's expression darkened. "Then we are finished. We have to be very careful about who we talk to and what we say. Test the waters first."

As the others began discussing ways to approach the townspeople, Iris drifted to the window, staring out at the quiet streets of Edenvale. The town looked as serene as ever, the perfectly manicured lawns glistening with morning dew. But now, every detail felt sinister—every shadow a potential threat, every smile a facade.

She clenched her fists, her mind racing with memories she couldn't fully grasp. The lab, the files, the voices—they swirled together like a storm, fragments that refused to form a clear picture. But one thing was certain: she had created this. And she had to end it.

"Iris." Sofia's voice broke through her thoughts, pulling her back to the present. "What do you think?"

Iris turned, meeting her friend's concerned gaze. "I think... we start small. Ask questions. Make them think without pushing too hard. If we can get even a few people to wake up, it'll create a ripple effect."

Mark nodded. "And we stay under the radar. No confrontations, no big moves. Just quiet whispers."

Elias stood, his chair scraping against the floor. "I'll leave now. The sooner I find Darnell, the better."

The forest surrounding Edenvale was unnaturally still as Elias made his way toward the hidden access point he'd used to enter the town. The tracking chip alarms wouldn't trigger for him, but that didn't mean he was safe. He kept to the shadows, his every step calculated and silent.

When he finally emerged beyond the boundaries of Edenvale, he paused, glancing back at the town's glowing lights in the distance. For a moment, doubt crept in. Could they really take down something so massive, so deeply entrenched? He shook the thought away and pressed on.

Hours later, he arrived. The small cabin was nestled in the shadows of towering pines, its weathered exterior almost camouflaged by the dense forest. Elias stepped onto the creaking porch, his breath visible in the cool night air. The faint glow from the window spilled onto the steps, and for a moment, he hesitated.

In The Shadow of Perfection

Then the door opened, and Darnell stood there, his familiar frame silhouetted against the warm light of the cabin's interior.

"Well, I'll be damned," Darnell said, a genuine smile breaking across his face. "You're a sight for sore eyes, Elias."

Elias stepped forward, his tension easing at the sight of his old friend. "Good to see you, too."

Darnell ushered him inside, his tone warm. "Come on, you must be freezing. And hungry. I've got stew on the stove."

The cabin's interior was as Elias remembered—cozy and cluttered, every surface bearing some sign of Darnell's lifelong tinkering. Tools, blueprints, and half-assembled gadgets covered the table, and the faint hum of hidden machinery added a layer of comfort.

As they sat at the table, bowls of steaming stew in front of them, Darnell's expression grew serious. "You didn't come all this way just for the company. What's going on, Elias?"

Elias leaned forward, his voice low. "Reynolds has gone too far, Darnell. He's turned Edenvale into a prison and a Petri dish, and I need your help to bring it down."

In The Shadow of Perfection

Darnell's face darkened. "I've suspected for a while. The man's lost the plot. This isn't what we signed up for." He sighed, running a hand through his hair. "You know I'm with you. Always have been. But what's the plan?"

Elias outlined their goals: the antidote, the power grid, and the bomb. At the mention of the bomb, Darnell's expression tightened.

"It's in the fountain," Darnell said after a long pause. "Right at the center of Edenvale. It's hidden in plain sight, built to look like part of the water filtration system. But Elias, listen to me—Reynolds wouldn't dare use it. Not unless everything spiraled out of control."

"Darnell, everything already has spiraled out of control," Elias said. "I can't just take that chance."

Darnell held up a hand. "I get it. I do. But the bomb isn't the immediate threat. The antidote and the power grid are. You take down the grid, you sever Edenvale from the lab. You get the antidote, you wake the people up. The bomb... we'll deal with it if we have to."

Elias leaned back, the tension in his shoulders easing slightly. "All right. Where's the antidote stored?"

Darnell gestured to the cluttered table. "I've got some old plans of the lab. The formula is stored in a secure vault, but I can get you a copy. As for the power grid, there's a central hub disguised as a maintenance building in the center of town. I'll draw up the schematics."

Elias exhaled, the weight of their task pressing heavily on him. "Thank you, Darnell. I don't know what I'd do without you."

Darnell smiled faintly. "You'd figure it out. You always do."

Over the next two days, Darnell housed Elias in the cabin, providing him with food, a warm bed, and a semblance of safety. They worked late into the night, poring over blueprints and schematics. Darnell's sharp mind was as focused as ever, his hands steady as he sketched out plans for cutting the power to Edenvale.

On the second night, as the fire crackled in the small hearth, Darnell handed Elias a notebook filled with his notes. "This has everything I can give you—the antidote formula, the layout of the power grid, and details on the bomb. It's encrypted, but you'll be able to crack it."

Elias accepted the notebook, his gratitude evident. "You've done more than enough, Darnell."

Darnell's expression softened. "We started this together, Elias. I'm not going to let Reynolds destroy everything we worked for."

In The Shadow of Perfection

Elias hesitated. "Why didn't you leave? You could have walked away."

Darnell laughed softly. "And go where? The world outside Edenvale isn't any kinder. At least here, I have a chance to make things right."

As dawn broke on the third day, Elias prepared to leave. Darnell stood on the porch, watching as his old friend packed the notebook and supplies into his bag.

"Be careful, Elias," Darnell said. "Reynolds isn't stupid. He'll know you're up to something."

Elias nodded. "I'll be back, Darnell. And when I am, we'll finish this."

Darnell's smile was small but genuine. "I'll hold you to that."

Elias stepped off the porch, the forest closing in around him as he disappeared into the trees. Darnell watched until he was gone, the weight of their mission settling heavily on his shoulders.

For the first time in years, Darnell felt a flicker of hope. They had a chance—a slim one, but a chance nonetheless—to set things right.

Meanwhile, back in Edenvale, Iris, Sofia, and Mark worked to execute their part of the plan. Iris took to the streets, engaging in seemingly casual conversations with the townspeople. She asked innocuous questions—"Do you ever feel like things are too perfect?" or "Do you ever wonder what life was like before Edenvale?"—planting seeds of doubt wherever she could.

Sofia used her social connections, hosting small gatherings and steering conversations toward memories and dreams. "Does anyone else have strange dreams? Ones that feel... too real?" she asked, her tone light but probing.

Mark kept a low profile, observing the town's routines and looking for cracks in Reynolds's control. He noticed small things—the bakery running out of flour, the fountain in the town square sputtering before resuming its perfect flow. The cracks were there, subtle but growing.

As the three worked, they couldn't shake the feeling that Reynolds was watching, waiting. Every time Iris passed a Shiny, she felt its blank gaze following her, even though the devices remained eerily silent. The silence was almost worse than the compliments—it was as if the Shinies were lying in wait.

Elias's voice echoed in her mind: *"We play the part. We smile and we follow the rules."*

In The Shadow of Perfection

But the act was growing harder with each passing day.

Chapter Thirty

Elias returned to Edenvale under the cover of darkness, slipping through the hidden forest path that bypassed the town's monitoring systems. The notebook Darnell had given him felt like a weight in his pack—both a burden and a beacon of hope.

The house was quiet when he arrived, the curtains drawn to block out prying eyes. He tapped on the back door in a specific rhythm, and within moments, Sofia answered. Her face lit with relief, but it was tempered by worry.

"You're back," she whispered, pulling him inside quickly. "Did you get it?"

Elias nodded, slipping the notebook from his pack and placing it on the dining table. Iris and Mark were already waiting, their expressions tense.

"What did you find?" Mark asked, his voice low but urgent.

In The Shadow of Perfection

Elias opened the notebook, spreading out the sketches and formulas Darnell had painstakingly included. "This," he said, pointing to a page filled with chemical notations, "is the formula for the antidote. And this," he gestured to a separate schematic, "is the layout of the central lab's storage vaults. If we follow these instructions, we can recreate the antidote and test it here."

Iris leaned forward, her fingers tracing the formula. A flicker of recognition crossed her face. "I wrote this," she murmured, almost to herself. "This was my work."

Sofia's hand rested on her friend's arm. "And now it's going to help us fix this."

The dining room became a makeshift lab. Elias unpacked the vials and chemicals Darnell had provided, arranging them carefully on the table. Iris's hands trembled as she picked up a pipette, memories of her days in the lab rushing back in fragmented flashes.

"I remember this," she said, her voice distant. "The balance of components, the way the solution has to be heated exactly to the right temperature... It's like muscle memory."

In The Shadow of Perfection

Sofia and Mark watched as Iris and Elias worked together, their movements methodical. The air was thick with concentration, every drop of liquid, every adjustment of the burner carrying an almost unbearable weight.

"What if it doesn't work?" Sofia whispered, her voice barely audible.

"It has to," Mark replied, though his tone betrayed his own doubt.

Finally, after hours of precise measurements and adjustments, Elias held up a vial of pale blue liquid. "This is it," he said, his voice filled with both hope and trepidation.

They all turned to Iris, who had volunteered to take the first dose. She stood, her hands steady as she accepted the vial from Elias. "If this works," she said, "we'll finally know the truth."

Sofia reached for her hand. "You don't have to do this alone."

Iris offered a faint smile. "I do. But thank you."

She tipped the vial back, the liquid cool and sharp as it slid down her throat. For a moment, nothing happened. Then, a rush of heat spread through her chest, radiating outward. She staggered, clutching the edge of the table as fragmented images flooded her mind.

A cozy home. A husband's laugh. Two children running through a sunlit yard.

Then, the crash—the shattering of glass, the world spinning, the screams. The ache of loss so profound it stole her breath.

Iris gasped, tears streaming down her face as she sank to her knees. "They were mine," she choked out. "My family... my children."

Sofia and Mark rushed to her side, but Elias held them back. "Give her a moment," he said gently. "The memories are coming back."

Iris's sobs eventually subsided, replaced by a quiet resolve. She looked up, her eyes fierce despite the tears. "I remember," she said. "And now I know why we have to stop Reynolds."

Sofia stepped forward, her expression a mix of fear and determination. "I'm next," she said.

Elias prepared another dose, handing her the vial with a solemn nod. "This will bring everything back. Are you ready?"

In The Shadow of Perfection

She hesitated, her hand trembling as she took the vial. "I need to know," she whispered, more to herself than anyone else. Then, without another word, she drank.

The reaction was immediate. Sofia clutched her stomach, a cry escaping her lips as her mind was flooded with memories.

A hospital room, sterile and cold. The beeping of monitors. A tiny, unmoving bundle in her arms. The unbearable grief of loss, again and again. The pills, the rope, the dark, suffocating despair.

Mark's voice broke through the haze, pleading with her to hold on. Promising her a new start. And then Edenvale—their perfect life, their perfect family. The children who weren't theirs, but whom she had grown to love as her own.

Sofia's knees buckled, and Mark caught her, holding her tightly as she wept. "I couldn't do it," she sobbed. "I couldn't face it anymore."

Mark's voice was thick with emotion. "I just wanted to save you, Sofia. I didn't know what else to do."

She pulled back, searching his face. "These kids we have now... they are not ours."

Mark hesitated, then shook his head. "No."

In The Shadow of Perfection

"Does that mean that someone could still take them away? Please tell me they can't take them away, I love them so much. I couldn't go through another loss," she asked as more tears rolled down her face.

"I legally adopted them before we came to Edenvale. We wanted to be parents; they needed parents; it seemed like the perfect fit," Mark said.

Sofia's tears came harder, a strange mix of pain and relief. "They're ours now," she said firmly. "And we'll protect them. No matter what. Which also means, not giving them the antidote, they were too little to understand anyway."

"She is right. Sometimes children don't remember parts of their past; the brain may have blocked traumatic incidents to protect them," said Iris.

The room fell into a heavy silence, broken only by the crackle of the fire. Elias placed a hand on Iris's shoulder, then Sofia's. "You both have your memories back now. You know what we're fighting for."

Sofia wiped her eyes, her expression hardening. "And we're not going to let Reynolds take this from anyone else."

Iris nodded, her voice steady despite the lingering pain. "We end this. Together."

In The Shadow of Perfection

The room held a charged silence, each of them absorbing the gravity of Iris's words.

Sofia broke the stillness, her voice low but resolute. "If we're going to wake everyone up, we'll need more antidote. A lot more."

Iris nodded, the scientist in her reignited. "I can replicate it, but we'll need time. And I'll need a proper space to work—somewhere secure, where no one will think to look."

Elias rubbed his jaw, his mind turning over possibilities. "There's an old maintenance shed near the woods on the outskirts of town. It is close enough though so it shouldn't set off the alarms. It hasn't been used in years, but I can get it ready. It'll be safe enough."

Mark leaned forward, his expression tight with concern. "That's one part of the plan. But shutting down the power grid? That's a whole different challenge. Edenvale's systems are heavily monitored. We'll have to be surgical."

Elias spread the schematics on the table, pointing to a cluster of nodes. "The main control hub is here, near the municipal building. If we can access this junction box, we can cut power to the entire town. It'll disable the Shinies and sever the connection to the lab."

In The Shadow of Perfection

Sofia frowned, tracing the map with her finger. "But won't that trigger alarms? If Reynolds knows what we're doing—"

"It's strange—we're talking about my father, but he doesn't seem like my father. Just weeks ago I would have bet he would never do anything to hurt me or anyone else. Now, I'm not so sure," Mark said sadly.

"We'll have to move quickly," Elias interrupted. "By the time he realizes what's happening, it'll already be too late."

Chapter Thirty-One

The following days were a blur of covert activity. Elias went in and out for supplies and chemicals. Under the guise of their usual routines, the group began preparing for their dual mission. Iris worked tirelessly in the makeshift lab, transforming the dilapidated shed into a functional workspace. The air inside was heavy with the scent of chemicals and the soft hum of burners. She fell into a rhythm, the process of creating the antidote unlocking fragments of her old life as a scientist.

Elias and Mark focused on the power grid, scouting the municipal building and noting security patterns. They discovered that the junction box was located in the basement, guarded by both physical locks and electronic surveillance.

"It's a fortress," Mark muttered as they studied the building from a nearby alley. "We'll need a distraction to get inside."

In The Shadow of Perfection

Elias's mind raced. "Leave that to me. I'll draw their attention while you handle the locks. Once you're in, it's just a matter of cutting the right cables."

Sofia, meanwhile, began planting seeds of doubt among the townspeople. At the café, in the market, during morning strolls—she dropped subtle hints, asking innocuous questions that made people pause and think.

"Do you ever wonder," she asked Mrs. Haverly one afternoon, "why no one ever leaves Edenvale? It's strange, isn't it? A place so perfect... yet so contained."

Mrs. Haverly laughed nervously, brushing off the comment. But later, Sofia caught her staring out the window, a frown creasing her brow.

When night came, the tension was palpable. They gathered in Iris's living room, their final plans laid out before them.

"I've prepared enough antidote for fifty people," Iris said, her voice steady despite the weight of her words. "It's not enough for the whole town, but it's a start."

Elias nodded. "We'll distribute it to those we trust first—the ones who'll help us wake the others. But we can't do that until the power is down."

In The Shadow of Perfection

Mark checked his watch. "The guards change shifts at midnight. That's our window."

Sofia reached for Iris's hand. "Are you ready for this?"

Iris looked at her, a flicker of fear in her eyes, quickly replaced by determination. "We don't have a choice."

Elias and Mark moved through the shadows, their footsteps muffled against the damp ground. The municipal building loomed ahead, its sterile exterior gleaming under the streetlights. They crouched behind a row of hedges, waiting for the guards to switch posts.

"Now," Elias whispered.

Mark slipped through the side entrance, a set of lockpicks in his hand. The physical lock yielded easily, but the electronic keypad required a bit more finesse. Beads of sweat formed on his brow as he worked, the seconds stretching into an eternity.

"Got it," he whispered, pushing the door open.

The basement was dimly lit, the hum of machinery filling the air. Elias stayed near the stairs, keeping watch, while Mark approached the junction box. He pulled out the diagram Elias had sketched and located the target cables.

In The Shadow of Perfection

His hands trembled as he reached for the wire cutters. "Are you sure about this?" he asked, glancing back at Elias.

Elias's jaw tightened. "Do it."

With a decisive snip, the cables severed. The hum of the machines stuttered and died, plunging the room into silence.

Back at Iris's house, the lights flickered and went out. Sofia lit a lantern, her heart pounding as she moved to the window. Outside, the streetlights had gone dark, and a strange stillness settled over the town.

"It's started," Iris said, her voice barely above a whisper.

They wasted no time, loading vials of the antidote into a small bag. Sofia and Iris moved through the town under cover of darkness, slipping the antidote into the hands of those they trusted—Rebecca, Mr. Bernard, Diana. Each person received the same instruction: "Take this when you're alone. Then come to Iris's house."

By dawn, a small group had gathered in Iris's living room—those who had already taken the antidote. Their reactions varied—some cried, some screamed, others sat in stunned silence as memories flooded back.

In The Shadow of Perfection

Rebecca was the first to speak. "I... I had a family," she whispered, tears streaming down her face. "A husband. Two little boys. I lost them in a fire..."

Her voice broke, and Sofia moved to her side, wrapping her in a comforting embrace. "You're not alone," she said. "We'll get through this together."

As the sun rose higher, the group began to form a plan. They would awaken more people, spreading the antidote like a ripple through the town. But they knew the risk—they were racing against time, and Reynolds would soon realize what was happening.

Elias stood at the center of the room, his voice firm. "We've taken the first step. But this is just the beginning. Reynolds won't let this go without a fight."

"And neither will we," Iris said, her voice strong. "This is our town. Our lives. And we'll take them back."

The group nodded, their fear replaced by a shared determination. They had woken up, and now it was time to wake the rest of them.

Chapter Thirty-Two

The sun rose over Edenvale, casting long golden rays that illuminated a town transformed. For the first time in years, the streets were alive with noise—real, raw, chaotic noise. People stood in groups on the sidewalks, their voices raised in confusion, anger, and disbelief. Without the Shinies murmuring their endless affirmations, without the soft hum of the town's power grid, Edenvale's once—perfect facade had crumbled.

Iris and Sofia stood on the porch of Iris's house, watching the commotion unfold. A woman down the street sobbed uncontrollably while clutching a photograph, her neighbors awkwardly trying to comfort her. A man paced back and forth in the square, muttering to himself as fragments of memory surfaced.

"This is chaos," Sofia said quietly, her voice tinged with unease. "People are remembering all at once. They're confused. Angry."

In The Shadow of Perfection

Iris nodded, her arms crossed tightly over her chest. "It was always going to be this way. The truth isn't easy."

Inside the house, Elias was hunched over a table covered in papers and files, meticulously sorting through schematics, antidote formulas, and surveillance notes. Mark sat across from him, his jaw tight, his eyes glued to the growing crowd outside.

Sofia turned back to them, her voice low but firm. "Something doesn't feel right. This has been... too easy. No one from the lab has tried to stop us."

Mark glanced at her, his expression cautious. "There's a reason for that. This is the time of year my father takes his two-week vacation. He's completely off the grid."

Sofia raised an eyebrow. "Your father? Off the grid? That doesn't sound like him."

Mark nodded, leaning back in his chair. "It's the one indulgence he allows himself. Every year, like clockwork. I don't know who's running the lab while he's gone, but—"

"Darnell," Elias interrupted, his voice steady. He looked up from his papers, his expression grim but resolute. "He is temporarily managing the lab. Reynolds put Darnell in charge while he's away—ironic, given Darnell's been sabotaging from the inside."

In The Shadow of Perfection

Sofia frowned. "Darnell? The guy who built the bomb?"

Elias gave a small, tight smile. "The very same. And right now, that's working in our favor."

Iris stepped inside, closing the door behind her to muffle the growing noise outside. "How is that possible?"

Elias leaned forward, his voice dropping. "Darnell has been working from the inside. He's spreading the truth among the lab staff, showing them what the Project has become. He's gaining their trust, building an alliance. By the time Reynolds gets back next week, Edenvale will be dismantled, and the people will be free."

Sofia crossed her arms, her brow furrowed. "Do you really think the staff will turn on Reynolds? He's controlled them for years."

Elias's gaze hardened. "They're scientists, not soldiers. Many of them were drawn to the Project for the same reasons I was—to help people. Darnell 's showing them how far Reynolds has strayed from that vision. And if enough of them side with us..."

Iris finished his thought, her voice strong. "We'll have the numbers to stop Reynolds for good."

In The Shadow of Perfection

The day passed in a whirlwind of activity. More people came to Iris's house, seeking answers, guidance, and solace. Rebecca arrived with a group of women from the market, each holding small items—trinkets from their past lives they had inexplicably kept. Mr. Bernard, once Edenvale's jovial handyman, arrived clutching a notebook filled with detailed sketches of machines. He had no memory of drawing them but knew instinctively they were important.

"People are waking up faster than we anticipated," Elias murmured as he watched the house fill with bodies and voices. "We'll need to move quickly if we're going to keep this momentum."

Sofia nodded, though her unease lingered. Something about the quiet from the lab didn't sit right with her. "What if Reynolds comes back early? What if he already suspects something?"

Elias shook his head. "Darnell would warn us. He's keeping us informed—"

A loud knock at the door silenced the room. Everyone froze, their eyes darting toward the sound.

Elias moved to the door cautiously, peering through the peephole. His shoulders tensed as he opened it, revealing Darnell standing on the porch, his face pale and drawn.

"You have to move faster," Darnell said without preamble, stepping inside and closing the door behind him. "Reynolds is coming back. Much sooner than expected."

Sofia's heart sank. "How soon?"

"Tomorrow," Darnell said grimly. "He wasn't supposed to be back until next week. He cut his vacation short. Someone—one of his loyalists—tipped him off that something was happening in Edenvale. He's furious."

Mark swore under his breath, running a hand through his hair. "That gives us less than twenty-four hours."

Darnell nodded, his expression urgent. "You have to act tonight. The power to the lab is still on, it runs separately from the town power grid. We have to shut it down tonight. Here is what you need to do: shut down the lab's systems, distribute the antidote—do whatever you can to make sure he has no control when he gets here. If he regains power..."

Sofia's voice was tight. "We are not going to let it happen."

In The Shadow of Perfection

Elias placed a hand on Darnell's shoulder. "What about you? Will you stay at the lab? If Reynolds finds out you've been helping us—"

Darnell's jaw tightened. "I'll handle Reynolds. You just focus on taking care of the town."

As darkness fell, the group gathered around the table one last time, their faces illuminated by the flickering firelight. The air was thick with tension, each of them acutely aware of the ticking clock.

Elias pointed to the map of Edenvale spread before them. "We hit the lab first. If we can disable their systems tonight, Reynolds won't be able to regain control. Iris and Sofia, you'll focus on distributing the rest of the antidote. Mark and I will handle the lab."

Sofia glanced at Darnell . "And you?"

Darnell's eyes flickered with something unreadable. "I'll make sure Reynolds doesn't have a chance to stop you."

The weight of his words settled over them, unspoken questions lingering in the air. No one asked what he meant, but they all understood the risks he was taking.

Iris clenched her fists, her voice steady despite the fear in her eyes. "We're ready."

In The Shadow of Perfection

Sofia placed a hand on her arm. "We've got this. Together."

Elias nodded. "Then let's move."

The group moved swiftly under the cover of darkness, each step heavy with purpose. Elias and Mark slipped through the shadows toward the lab, their breaths quiet but measured. Sofia and Iris moved in the opposite direction, their bags heavy with vials of the antidote.

As the town fell into a restless silence, a black car rolled to a stop at the edge of Edenvale. The headlights flicked off, and the driver stepped out, his polished shoes crunching against the gravel.

Reynolds adjusted his coat, his sharp gaze sweeping over the town. A slow, cold smile spread across his face as he murmured to himself, "Let's see what you've been up to, Dr. Corwin."

Chapter Thirty-Three

Reynolds adjusted his tie as he stepped out of his sleek black car, the dim moonlight casting a silvery glow on the eerily quiet streets of Edenvale. The power outage had plunged the town into an unsettling stillness, broken only by the occasional murmur of voices from distant homes. He walked slowly, his polished shoes clicking against the pavement, his sharp eyes taking in every detail—the absence of the faint hum of the Shinies, the restless energy in the air. This was no longer the perfect Edenvale he had controlled. It was chaos.

No Shinies, no cameras—but patterns are a surveillance too, he thought to himself. *You always come back here.* Stopping in front of Sofia's house, Reynolds tilted his head, the shadow of a smirk playing at his lips. So, *this is where it all began to unravel,* he thought. The power outage had killed the smart locks; so the latch slid under his hand. Without hesitation, he opened the door and stepped inside.

In The Shadow of Perfection

The room was dark, the furniture cast in shadow, but the faint scent of woodsmoke lingered—a sign of recent activity. He moved silently, settling into a chair in the corner of the living room, his presence a chilling reminder of the control he once wielded.

Near midnight, after hours spent in the dark town, the four returned to Sofia's house, their footsteps weary but purposeful. Iris's face was streaked with dirt, her hands still clutching the remnants of her notes. Elias carried the weight of the group's hope, fresh vials and Darnell's schematics secured in a pouch slung over his shoulder. Mark walked beside Sofia, his expression grim, his mind racing with possibilities and doubts.

As they stepped into the house, the oppressive silence hit them like a wall. Iris flicked on a flashlight, the beam cutting through the darkness. The light landed on Reynolds, seated calmly in the corner, his hands resting on the arms of the chair.

"Good evening," he said, his voice low and measured. "Quite the busy day you've had."

Sofia gasped, instinctively stepping back. "Reynolds."

Elias moved forward, placing himself protectively between Reynolds and the group. "You shouldn't be here."

In The Shadow of Perfection

Reynolds chuckled, a hollow sound that sent shivers down their spines. "Oh, Elias, this is my Project. I can be wherever I want. The better question is, what do you all think you're doing?"

Mark stepped forward, his fists clenched. "We're undoing the mess you've made."

Reynolds's gaze flicked to Mark, his expression unreadable. "And you, my son. Betraying your own father. I expected better."

Mark didn't flinch. "You're not the man I thought you were. You've turned this into something monstrous."

Reynolds's face hardened, his tone cutting. "What I've done is preserve lives. Lives that would have been lost to grief, despair, and self-destruction. Do you think these people are ready to face the real world again? Look around you—this town is falling apart because of your meddling."

Iris stepped forward, her voice trembling but resolute. "You're wrong. The people want their lives back. They're remembering who they are, and they're ready to fight for their freedom."

Reynolds stood, his presence suddenly towering. "Freedom? Freedom to return to pain? To struggle? You call that freedom? I created a sanctuary here, a place where no one has to hurt again."

"You created a prison," Sofia snapped, her voice filled with fury. "You stripped people of their memories, their identities. You erased who they were."

Reynolds reached into his pocket, pulling out a small, matte-black remote—a single recessed button. The fountain's fail-safe.

"I won't let you destroy what I've built," Reynolds said, his voice cold. "One press, and Edenvale ceases to exist. This town, these people—they'll all disappear. Don't think I won't do it."

Elias stepped forward, his hands raised in a gesture of calm. "Reynolds, listen to yourself. You're threatening the very lives you claim to have saved. This isn't preservation. It's tyranny."

Reynolds's finger hovered over the button, his expression unyielding. "You've given these people nothing but chaos. They're scared, confused. They need order."

"They need the truth," Iris countered, her voice firm. "Most of them have families, friends—people who've been missing them. They deserve to know the truth. And they're ready. They've already faced their pain and found a way to heal. You don't get to take that from them."

Reynolds's hand trembled slightly, the first crack in his composure. "You think you know better? You think you can just undo this? You have no idea what you're dealing with."

A voice came from the shadows, calm but laced with authority. "And neither do you anymore."

The group turned as Darnell stepped into the room, his presence both reassuring and unsettling. His sharp eyes locked on Reynolds, and for the first time, the doctor's confidence seemed to waver.

"Darnell." Reynolds said, his tone a mix of anger and surprise. "I should've known you were involved."

Darnell crossed his arms, his expression unreadable. "You lost your way, Reynolds. This was never meant to be about control."

Reynolds straightened, regaining some of his composure. "You're a traitor. Everything we've built—"

"Everything you've twisted," Darnell interrupted, his voice cutting. "This Project was about healing, not manipulation. You've turned it into a nightmare."

In The Shadow of Perfection

Reynolds's gaze darted between Darnell and the group, his grip tightening on the detonator. "You think you can stop me?"

Darnell stepped closer, his tone steady. "I know we can. You're outnumbered, Reynolds. The people are waking up. They know the truth. And soon, you won't have anyone left to manipulate."

The tension in the room was palpable as Reynolds weighed his options, the weight of his decisions written across his face.

"Put it down, Dad," Mark said, his voice softer now, almost pleading. "It's over."

Reynolds's hand faltered, the device shaking slightly in his grasp. For a moment, the room seemed to hold its breath. Somewhere in the quiet, the fireplace ticked as it cooled. He held the detonator tightly, his knuckles white, a man teetering on the edge of madness.

Elias stepped forward, his voice low but firm. "Reynolds, where are they? The people who disappeared. What did you do to them?"

Reynolds sneered, a cold, hollow laugh escaping his lips. "You think you want to know, Elias, but you don't."

In The Shadow of Perfection

Elias's fists clenched. "Tell me. You owe them that much."

Reynolds's smirk faded, replaced by something darker, more insidious. "Fine. You want the truth? They're gone. So, we had to dispose of them."

"What do you mean they're gone?" Elias barked, demanding an answer that would satisfy no one.

"They didn't make it."

Chapter Thirty-Four

The room fell silent. Iris felt her knees weaken, and Sofia gripped the edge of the table, her knuckles pale. "Didn't make it?" Sofia's voice trembled, disbelief and horror mingling. "What does that mean?"

"Do I have to spell it out for you, sweetheart? They were tests," Reynolds said coldly. "Failures, all of them. They couldn't handle the reintegration process. Their minds broke down. Their bodies followed."

Elias's jaw tightened as he struggled to keep his composure. "You experimented on them? Without their consent? You turned them into lab rats."

Reynolds's gaze flickered to him, unrepentant. "It's called science, Elias. Progress doesn't come without sacrifice."

Sofia shook her head, tears filling her eyes. "You're talking about lives—human lives—as if they're disposable."

In The Shadow of Perfection

"They were already broken," Reynolds snapped. "They came here because they had nothing left. We gave them a chance to start over, and when they failed… they ceased to be our concern."

"Your concern?" Elias echoed, his voice trembling with fury. "You played god with their lives, and when it didn't suit your experiment, you erased them."

Reynolds smirked, unashamed. "It was for the greater good."

Iris stepped forward, her voice trembling but fierce. "They were people, Reynolds. They trusted you. They trusted me. And you betrayed that trust."

Reynolds's mask of calm cracked, his voice rising. "And what would you have done, Iris? Hm? Left them to wallow in their misery? To destroy themselves? At least I gave them a chance."

"A chance?" Elias's voice was sharp, cutting through Reynolds's tirade. "You gave them false hope and then discarded them when they didn't fit your vision. You're no scientist—you're a butcher."

Reynolds's face twisted with rage. "Don't you dare lecture me, Elias. You wouldn't understand the pressure, the responsibility of this Project. I kept Edenvale alive. I kept control."

In The Shadow of Perfection

Elias stepped closer, his voice a low growl. "And in doing so, you killed the very thing it was meant to protect: humanity."

Reynolds slammed his hand against the table, the detonator trembling in his grasp. "You think you can take this from me? You think you can destroy everything I've built?"

"No," Darnell said, his voice calm but resolute. "You've already done that yourself."

Reynolds's head snapped toward him, his eyes blazing. "Careful, Darnell."

Darnell stepped forward, unflinching. "You've lost control, Reynolds. Look at yourself. You're a man with nothing left but a button."

"Don't push me," Reynolds warned, his voice a dangerous growl.

Darnell smirked, his tone sharp and deliberate. "Push it, then. Do it. Show us how far you've fallen. You are so lost, you don't even know what you're holding."

Elias's heart pounded. "Darnell, stop! We have to be careful and reasonable."

But Darnell didn't back down. "If you're so certain you're right, Reynolds, go ahead. Prove it."

In The Shadow of Perfection

Reynolds's hand wavered over the button, his breathing ragged. "Don't think I won't."

"Then do it!" Darnell shouted, his voice echoing through the room. "But know this: you won't just be destroying Edenvale. You'll be destroying yourself too." Darnell turned to the others; his face etched with determination. "Get out. All of you. Leave now! Go! Get everyone away from the fountain."

Sofia hesitated, her eyes wide with fear. "Darnell..."

"Go! Reynolds and I can settle this, but in the meantime you need to keep the rest of the people safe. Go!" Darnell barked, his voice leaving no room for argument.

The four bolted out of the house, their footsteps pounding against the pavement as they raced toward the center of town. The fountain loomed ahead, its serene waters glistening under the moonlight.

"Everyone, move!" Sofia yelled, her voice cracking with urgency. "Get away from the fountain. Now!"

Confusion rippled through the crowd as people began to scatter. Mark and Elias ushered them away, their voices rising above the growing panic.

"What's he doing?" Iris gasped, clutching Sofia's arm.

Elias's face was grim. "Darnell is buying us time."

In The Shadow of Perfection

A deafening explosion shattered the night, the ground trembling beneath their feet. A plume of fire and smoke rose in the distance, illuminating the town in a fiery glow.

"No!" Sofia whispered, her voice breaking.

Iris clung to Elias, tears streaming down her face. "Darnell..."

The crowd fell silent, their eyes fixed on the inferno where Sofia's house had once stood.

Elias's voice was barely audible. "The bomb wasn't in the fountain like he told us. It was in the detonator."

"What? You knew?" Iris was stunned.

"Yes." He swallowed. "He re-keyed that transmitter a few days ago—to a shaped charge under the living-room floor. It was also part of the plan to lead Reynolds to Sofia's house for this very reason," he exhaled. "If it ever came down to destroying the town, Darnell wanted the one who pushed the button to be the first to pay."

Heat slapped their backs; a fine grit of glass ticked across the cobbles. Somewhere a child cried; then only the hiss and crackle of the blaze.

In The Shadow of Perfection

Iris's voice broke. "Oh, Darnell. He sent us to the fountain so we'd be out of the house. All the while knowing he was not going to come out alive."

Sofia nodded, tears catching in the firelight. "At least no one else was inside." She drew a shaky breath. "Emma and Caleb are at Rebecca's for a sleepover. I've been keeping them away from all of this."

The fire was burning slowly, a beacon of loss and defiance. Reynolds was gone, along with his twisted vision for Edenvale. But the fight wasn't over. The people had awakened, and the truth could no longer be silenced.

Chapter Thirty-Five

The morning light broke over Edenvale, casting a golden hue over the once-frozen town. The air, for the first time in years, felt real—unfiltered, unmonitored. The hum of Edenvale's hidden machinery was gone, leaving only the sound of birdsong and the soft murmur of awakening voices.

The people were free.

As the townsfolk gathered in the square, they looked around at each other, no longer bound by the glossy veneers of their former lives. Their faces were etched with emotions they hadn't dared to feel in years— confusion, fear, hope. Once the centerpiece of Edenvale's manufactured serenity, the fountain now stood as a symbol of resilience, its waters shimmering in the sunlight over a simple plaque that read, 'DARNELL. THANK YOU.

Sofia stood with Mark, their adopted children clinging to their sides. The weight of the last few days hung over them, but there was a lightness too—a sense of possibility. Sofia knelt down, brushing a stray curl from her daughter's face. "You're free now," she whispered, her voice trembling. "We all are."

The girl's wide eyes sparkled with innocence. "What does that mean, Mommy?"

"It means we get to make our own choices," Mark said, his voice steady. "We get to decide who we want to be and where we want to go."

Caleb looked up at him, his small hands clutching Mark's shirt. "Even if we don't stay here?"

Mark nodded, his throat tightening. "Especially if we don't stay here."

Sofia's gaze drifted to the crowd, where people were beginning to talk, their voices rising with the energy of rediscovery. A man embraced a woman, tears streaming down their faces as they exchanged names they hadn't spoken in years. A mother clutched a photo of a child she had forgotten, her sobs breaking the stillness.

Sofia and Mark packed whatever was left of their belongings, their children running excitedly. The weight of their shared pain had lifted, replaced by a cautious optimism. They had decided to move to a small town near the coast, a place where they could start anew.

As Sofia folded the last of the clothes into a suitcase, Mark wrapped his arms around her from behind. "How are you?" he asked softly.

She leaned into him, her eyes closing. "For the first time in a long time, I think I can finally say: I'm okay."

Their daughter, Emma, peeked around the door, a wide grin on her face. "Mommy, Daddy, can we get a dog when we move?"

Mark chuckled, pressing a kiss to Sofia's temple. "What do you think?"

Sofia laughed, a genuine, unrestrained sound. "I think a dog sounds perfect."

The days that followed were a blur of departures and reunions. Families who had been separated by the Project found each other again, their joy mingling with the bittersweet reality of what they had lost. Letters and calls flooded in from the outside world as Edenvale's participants reconnected with their pasts.

At the edge of town, Iris and Elias watched as the last of the power lines came down. The town was quiet now, a shell of what it had been, but its silence felt peaceful rather than oppressive.

"Are you okay?" Elias asked.

She glanced up at him, her expression softening. "I think so," she said. "It's overwhelming. All these people... all these lives we've disrupted."

Elias stepped closer, his voice gentle. "We didn't disrupt them, Iris. We set them free."

She turned to face him fully, her eyes searching his. "And what about us? What happens now?"

For a moment, Elias didn't answer. He looked at her as if seeing her for the first time, the woman who had once envisioned Edenvale as a sanctuary for the broken. "I don't know what happens next," he admitted. "But I know I want to face it with you."

Iris's breath caught, her heart pounding. "Elias..."

"You were the heart of this Project," he said, his voice thick with emotion. "And even when it was twisted into something else, you never lost that. You gave people hope, Iris. And you've given me hope."

Tears welled in her eyes as she reached for his hand. "I don't know if I'm ready for this. For us."

In The Shadow of Perfection

He squeezed her hand gently. "Neither am I. But maybe that's the point. We take it one step at a time."

Iris nodded, a small, tentative smile breaking through the uncertainty. "One step at a time."

As the sun dipped below the horizon, casting the town in a golden glow, the two of them stood together, their hearts lighter, their paths uncertain but finally their own.

Edenvale had been a place of illusions, of pain, and of healing. But now, it was a place of beginnings—a place where the broken could rebuild, and where hope, no matter how faint, could always find its way back.

www.ingramcontent.com/pod-product-compliance
Lightning Source LLC
Chambersburg PA
CBHW020056180626
46812CB00006B/2351